The Academy
GAME ON

The Academy
GAME ON

MONICA SELES

and James LaRosa

BLOOMSBURY

NEW YORK   LONDON   NEW DELHI   SYDNEY

First published in the United States of America in June 2013
by Bloomsbury Children's Books
www.bloomsbury.com

For information about permission to reproduce selections from this book, write to
Permissions, Bloomsbury Children's Books, 175 Fifth Avenue, New York, New York 10010

Library of Congress Cataloging-in-Publication Data
Seles, Monica.
Game on / by Monica Seles. — First U.S. edition.
pages   cm. — (The Academy ; 1)
Summary: Sixteen-year-old tennis star Maya's dreams come true when she earns a scholarship to
the Academy, a sports training facility/boarding school for teenaged athletes, but can she survive
the constant drama of her talented classmates?
ISBN 978-1-59990-901-1 (paperback) • ISBN 978-1-59990-976-9 (hardcover)
ISBN 978-1-61963-005-5 (e-book)
[1. Athletes—Fiction. 2. Tennis—Fiction. 3. Dating (Social customs)—Fiction. 4. Interpersonal
relations—Fiction.] I. Title.
PZ7.S456918Gam 2013   [Fic]—dc23   2012038359

Book design by Nicole Gastonguay
Typeset by Westchester Book Composition
Printed in the U.S.A. by Thomson-Shore, Dexter, Michigan
2 4 6 8 10 9 7 5 3 1 (paperback)
2 4 6 8 10 9 7 5 3 1 (hardcover)

All papers used by Bloomsbury Publishing, Inc., are natural, recyclable products
made from wood grown in well-managed forests. The manufacturing processes
conform to the environmental regulations of the country of origin.

To all the people who have helped me on my varied paths through life and to the fans and friends who have allowed all the twists and turns

The Academy
GAME ON

Chapter 1

Even though the bus smelled like Pringles and gym socks, it was the single greatest ride of Maya's life. Sure, she was the pillow for an old woman for most of the last twenty-three hours (Maya had sworn she was dead around Richmond), but she was finally here. She was here! And as she stepped off the bus and stood at the gates that opened to her final destination, the feeling that nearly knocked her out of her sneakers could be summed up in a single word: run.

Run? Was she insane? Everything she'd ever wanted—everything she'd worked so hard for—was on the other side of these gates. Maya couldn't count the number of birthday candles, wishing-well coins, and wishbones that were sacrificed so that she could be standing on this very spot at this very moment. Nerves is all this was. And who would blame her? Beyond these gates, her life was about to change forever.

Maya had arrived at the Academy.

The Academy was, without question, the greatest sports training facility in the world. It was responsible for more Olympic gold medalists, Hall of Famers, and number-one-ranked professional athletes than anywhere else on earth. The place was a factory, and its lone product was champions. Maya's dream was to be one of them.

Even with all the competing Maya had done in her life, her hardest fight had been getting into the Academy. There were only two ways in: an obscene amount of talent or an obscene amount of cash. And even then, admission wasn't a guarantee. There was a waiting list to get on the waiting list. Because Maya's family was more or less broke, her only hope had been to earn a scholarship.

The first year she tried out for one, the rejection was a disappointment. The second year, she cried in front of the recruiter. The third year, she didn't come out of her room for a week. On the fourth try, she was so used to the official rejection that she started mouthing the words as the recruiter spoke. Maya was blown away when he'd actually started saying something different. Finally, she had done it. This sixteen-year-old have-not from central New York with absolutely no connections whatsoever had somehow made it into the *most* exclusive club. To this moment she still thought it might be a giant practical joke.

As tough as it was to get in, it had been almost as tough for Maya to leave home. She wasn't one of those kids who hated their parents. Her mother and father didn't know the first thing about tennis, but they supported her 100 percent. They didn't have much money, but whatever they had they invested in her. In her dream. She never felt the need to rebel. What was there to rebel against? So the scene at the station, when she'd loaded her last suitcase under the bus, had been a hot mess.

There were tears, hugs, and fistfuls of cash and coins shoved into her pockets like she was a Thanksgiving turkey. Her mother made her promise to call her every day, any time she got injured, and the second she even thought she might be coming down with something. Her father warned her about guys and threatened to beat up anyone who hurt his baby, which was ludicrous since (a) Maya had never so much as brought a guy home and (b) the only thing her father fought was the battle of the bulge.

"Name?" The guard stared down at her from his post at the gates.

"Hart, Maya Hart." Was she screaming? She felt like she was screaming. She watched the guard enter her name into the system. With his pencil-thin mustache and his uniform starched to tortured perfection, he resembled a cop more than campus security. After what felt like an eternity, his printer started to whir. It wasn't a practical joke after all—she was in the system. He handed her a pass.

"Take this to Admissions. Welcome to the Academy, Maya Hart." He opened the gates. Maya swallowed hard. She grabbed her bags, took a deep breath . . . and walked inside.

Maya stood in the main office with a welcome packet that practically weighed more than she did. The sheer number of things she had to sign off on receiving before getting her dorm key was staggering. Maps, class schedules, rules, regulations, safety precautions, emergency contact numbers, codes of conduct, nondisclosure agreements . . . (Maya didn't even know what a nondisclosure agreement was, but she'd sign anything to get that key.) Finally, it was placed in her hand. As she looked down at it, this key she had dreamed about since she was in single digits, she knew she wouldn't hesitate to bite the fingers off anyone who tried to take it from her.

But she wasn't fast enough.

"Hey!" Maya turned, ready to take action. Her eyes went wide. Staring her dead in the face was none other than three-time Super Bowl MVP Nails Reed. Nails was a quarterback and a living legend—six foot four, square-jawed, and an idol to millions (including Maya's father). But he was most important to her as the owner of the Academy. He made the *final* decisions on who came. And who went.

"Watson twenty-six, huh?" he said, reading her key. "You're the new girl. Persistent, from what I hear."

"Maya Hart," she said. Was she supposed to gush over him? Act nonchalant? Compliment his hair? The most famous person she'd met before him was the guy who played the grapes in the Fruit of the Loom commercials. Truth be told, that was probably the greatest day of her life until now.

"Your folks parking the car?" By his tone it was clear that most kids didn't arrive solo.

"They couldn't get off work." For the first time, Maya was relieved about that. Her dad would've been riding Nails piggyback up and down the hallway and regurgitating stats even Nails himself didn't know.

Nails looked around her. "Where's the rest of your stuff?"

"This is it," she replied. She had two suitcases and a tennis bag, which she'd felt fully confident with until this very moment. She waited for him to say something that would make her feel better about it.

"Follow me." *Okay, maybe not.* He walked on. Maya didn't hesitate. She grabbed her stuff and, like a shot, took off after him.

He held the rear door of the Admissions building open. Sunlight flooded in. If Maya's mind wasn't blown before, it was definitely blown now. Like Dorothy Gale from Kansas, she stepped out from black and white into color. She was in Oz.

And by the looks of it, Oz didn't come cheap.

The Academy wasn't a sweat-stained training ground; it was a resort. Office buildings were bungalows, and dorms were million-dollar villas with Mercedes and BMWs lined up out front, pristine and sparkling clean as if driven here directly off the lot. The pool to her right came complete with cabanas and an attendant. Up ahead, there was a cluster of stores, from Hermès and Versace to Prada and Manolo Blahnik, with an Aveda spa sandwiched in between.

Trees and lanterns lined every pathway. Fountains and flowers dotted every lawn. It made the Garden of Eden look like a weed-infested parking lot, which, coincidentally, was the view from Maya's bedroom window back home. Throughout was the most impressive sight of all: half-dressed, hard-bodied guys and girls soaking up the sun, modeling their six-hundred-dollar Chanel shades and designer swimsuits, and strutting around like the glorious, God-gifted peacocks they were. All Maya could think was, *Sports happen here?*

"We want the Academy to be your world," Nails said. "So we've made sure everything you could possibly want or need is right here on this campus."

"How about a trust fund?" Maya said with a laugh.

Nails didn't offer so much as a smile. "When you're good, that's not a problem for long." She couldn't tell if it was an endorsement or a warning. She didn't remember Nails being this serious in his Slim Jim commercial.

They continued their tour. He told her about the amenities, the on-campus high school, the facilities, the famous athletes whose sweat was soaked into every square inch of the place. The fifty-two tennis courts, the two golf courses, the Olympic-sized swimming pool, the basketball courts . . . Around every corner was something new to take her breath away. A 24-karat baseball diamond, a state-of-the-art track field. Even the building used for classes made Maya actually want to go. They approached a football field that was so meticulously manicured that it looked fake. On it was one serious pickup game. Maya spotted someone watching the game from the stands. Someone familiar.

"Wait," Maya said, looking at him. "Isn't that . . . ?" She sharpened her focus. "It is! That's what's-his-name from that disaster movie, the one where the guy has twenty-four hours to stop the moon from crashing into the earth! Does he have a kid who goes here?"

"Celebrities come here all the time," Nails said, unimpressed. "Hollywood is where people go to gawk at stars. The Academy is where stars come to do their gawking. They're either here to see our alums who keep this place as their home base or they're coming to see what superstars are around the corner. You better get used to it, fast."

Maya nodded emphatically. But she had no idea how anyone could ever get used to that. *Why would you even want to?*

Nails flagged down one of the guys on the field. The quarterback. Everyone stopped midplay so the kid could run over to them. As he got closer, Maya froze. Broad-shouldered, cleancut, dimples for days. He was without a doubt the most beautiful specimen of man she'd ever seen.

"My son Travis," Nails said as he was nearly to them. *Of course*, Maya thought. In addition to being physically flawless, he had to be filthy rich, too. Maya suddenly became acutely aware that she'd spent the last day on a bus marinating in other people's funk.

"Travis, you're not stepping into your throw enough," Nails told him when he'd reached them. "You should be sixty percent on your front foot when you're releasing the ball."

"Like this?" Travis asked. He tried to work out the motion, but his father had to step in and adjust his weight for him. Travis was more than happy for the correction. It was clear by the reverence he had for his father that Travis wasn't an unwilling Mini-Me. As they continued to perfect the motion, Maya couldn't help but think she would've ventured off the tennis court more often if she knew guys like Travis Reed roamed the earth. As it was, she had no idea what to say or how to react if he ever looked her way.

Suddenly, he was looking her way.

And smiling!

God, he was beautiful. And she was frozen. She had no idea how long it was before he ran back to his game. A moment? An hour? It was just a brief, polite smile, but it was enough to make Maya swoon out of her socks. If only . . .

"You coming or not?" Nails was waiting for her to continue their walk. Oh, God, she thought, how long had she been staring? Did he notice? She bolted from her spot to catch up.

After a few more sights that Maya couldn't even concentrate on, they wound up at a strange place. It was almost like they'd crossed some imaginary border. The buildings were somewhat less impressive, the surroundings not quite as pretty as a postcard.

"Watson Hall, this is your stop." Nails motioned to her new home.

"Where's the Hermès store?" Maya asked. She always joked when she was nervous. By the blank expression looking back at her, she knew Nails was not one to be joked with. "Thank you so much," she said, eager to move on. "My father will flip when I tell him I got my tour of the campus from *the* Nails Reed."

"Tour?" Nails asked. "I don't give tours. This was just on the way to a meeting. Ms. Hart, this campus is six hundred acres. It's up to you to figure it out."

"Oh," she said. Her VIP tour suddenly felt a lot less VIP.

"Um, before you go, I just wanted to say . . . being here is . . . being here is an absolute dream come true. People say that, but . . . for me, it is. And I won't take a second of it—not a single second—for granted. And I am persistent. I want to be the number-one player in the world, and I'm going to get there." She wasn't usually so direct, but she was being genuine. It felt right. And she felt powerful saying it.

Nails was as unmoved by her statement as he was by the movie star they'd passed earlier. "Everyone wants to be number one here," he said. "Everyone's a phenom. That's why our scholarships are provisional. You have six months to prove you not only want to be a star, but also that you have the goods to pull it off. Six months, or you're out. Have a nice day." With that, he was gone.

As Maya stood there alone, the fear that overwhelmed her outside the gates returned. It pounded her like a wave. But this time, she understood it. After fighting like a dog to get in, after busing down the entire eastern seaboard to get here, that urge to run was really the intense and all-too-familiar feeling that she didn't belong. That Maya might quite possibly be in way over her head.

Chapter 2

At the first sign of trouble, Maya always turned to her mother. When girls kept chanting "Bigfoot" at her in fifth grade (Maya grew five inches that year) and when her tennis skirt split up the back during the finals of the Spring Invitational (showing everyone in the stands London, France, and half of Barcelona), her mother had been her rock. She might not have always been able to solve the problem, but just being there to listen made Maya feel better. After Maya's antipep talk by Nails filled her with molten dread, her mother was the one person she *couldn't* talk to. Her mother had already been so worried about sending Maya out on her own, so Maya didn't want to put the woman in the hospital with one phone call. As Maya walked up the stairs to her dorm room, she felt not only incredibly anxious, but also incredibly alone.

She reached the door to her room. Even if it wasn't

Shangri-la, she thought, imagining what could be on the other side, it was hers. At least for the next six months, she'd have someplace calm and relaxing to retreat to. What she found when she opened the door, however, was what could only be described as a crime scene.

The two beds were stripped bare. There were ransacked closets, opened drawers—and towels covered in fresh red handprints. What on earth had happened in here?

Maya started to poke through the debris on a desk when the door closed hard behind her. She turned, startled, and found an Asian girl with a towel wrapped around her head. Her hands were covered in red.

"Are you the new roommate?" The way the girl asked, so monotonic, was almost as unsettling as every other ounce of this moment.

"Uh, I'm not sure," Maya responded hesitatingly. "What happened to the last one?"

"I caught her looking through my things and had to kill her," she said bluntly. Maya just stared, her hand still wrist-deep in this girl's stuff. "Oh, relax." The girl laughed. "I was just dying my hair." She undid the towel. Sure enough, half of her hair was red; the other half was shaved completely. "Last week was blue, the week before, purple."

Maya touched her own plain blond hair and eased up only slightly. "What about the closets, the drawers . . . ?"

"That's just how I live," she said matter-of-factly. "Are you okay with that?" She tossed her towel onto the floor.

"Do I have a choice?" Maya asked.

The girl's reply came back swift and flat. "No."

"Then, sure, I'm totally okay with that." Maya smiled as if to say, *See, I can banter. We're bantering. Please like me.*

"I'm Li Sun," she said, still in monotone. "My friends call me Cleo." Maya wasn't sure which category she was being put into.

"You're a golfer," Maya said. The only thing not thrown about the room was a set of golf clubs. They were spotless, with spotless white golf club covers, and were propped up in a spotless white golf bag.

"I am," Cleo said. "You know anything about golf?"

Maya thought hard. Lie or tell the truth, lie or tell the truth? "Not a thing," she finally confessed.

"Good. I don't know a thing about tennis," Cleo said, motioning to Maya's rackets. "So we won't have to bore each other with all that crap." Cleo was nothing if not blunt. Maya got the sense that it was meant to be off-putting, but she sort of liked it.

"Is everyone in Watson a scholarship kid?" Maya asked.

"Welcome to the projects, baby," Cleo said, loading her ear with earrings. "Watson is for all the poor saps born in the real world. What we lack in trust funds and celebrity parents, we more than make up for in pluck and the ability to digest ramen noodles for breakfast, lunch, and dinner."

Maya laughed. Cleo eyed her, but her look said, *Okay, she's got some kind of brain.* Maya thought this would've bought her some slack, but instead Cleo focused even harder on her.

"How did you get into tennis?" Cleo asked—well, not so much *asked* as *demanded.*

"Well," Maya responded, "when I was seven, I found a tennis racket in my next-door neighbor's stuff."

"In their stuff?" Cleo asked. "You a thief?"

"No," Maya said, hesitating. Finally, she confessed. "In their trash."

"Hm," Cleo said. For some reason, that seemed to please her. "Go on."

"Um, it was the middle of winter, so all I did with it was hit icy snowballs. Pretty soon, I was able to knock out all eight windows in the garage door, on purpose. Since it was cheaper to pay for tennis lessons than to keep replacing the windows, my parents used their savings to enroll me in classes. I've basically been on a tennis court ever since."

Cleo began circling her. "Twenty-four-seven, huh?"

Maya eyed her. "Yeah."

"Must've sucked when all the other kids were hanging out at the mall. Or hooking up at parties . . ."

This was clearly a test. Maya didn't know the rules or what it took to pass it. So she stuck to being honest.

"I used to complain about it," Maya said. "But deep down, I sort of knew: The court wasn't a prison. It was a hideout."

Cleo leaned back. She seemed . . . satisfied.

"How long have you been at the Academy?" Maya asked, eager to shift the focus.

"Eight months," Cleo replied. "The US, five years. Took me a while to get settled in the States before I tried out for this place."

Maya nodded. "Took me four years of trying to get in."

Cleo looked at Maya. "It took me four years, too," she said

finally. "Maybe don't tell other people that, though. It could be interpreted as a sign of weakness, and that doesn't go over too well here. That and Crocs, even if you wear them ironically."

Maya smiled. Cleo was now trusting her with private details. "You passed the six-month probationary period," Maya said. "You must be doing something right."

Cleo laughed. "There is no six-month probationary period."

Maya was confused. "I just talked to Nails Reed; he told me—"

"Oh, honey," Cleo said. "Here's a little secret from me to you. It never ends. The minute you're not up to par, you're out on your behind."

"Are you serious?" Maya didn't come all this way to have to turn right back around.

"You know how long my last roommate was here?" Cleo asked. "Three months. The one before that? Three weeks. They either jump back on a bus or jump in front of one."

"You're lying."

"You're right," Cleo said. "Some are pushed."

Maya chewed on her lip. She decided that the first step to her survival was to knock this whole subject out of her head.

"You're tough," Maya said. "You're hanging on."

"I don't have a choice," Cleo said blandly. "I've got an entire family back home in China with nothing. Less than nothing. I either make this happen or . . ." Cleo didn't seem eager to see that thought through.

"Must be a lot of pressure," Maya said. Cleo didn't

respond. Maya didn't want to press it. "I can't believe you've only been in the States five years. Your English is better than mine."

"Don't get me wrong," Cleo said, kicking her things away from Maya's bed. "When I'm in China, you'd think you plucked me straight from the rice fields. But if you want to be an international brand, you need to talk like you were born in the Mall of America."

"Hard to see you blending in on the rice fields with that hair," Maya joked. "Or the Mall of America. Or a golf course, for that matter. I don't think I've ever seen a punked-out golfer before."

"That's because there are none," Cleo said, a hint of wistfulness weighing down her words. Maya had inadvertently touched something off in her. "I'm going to have to think about that if I'm lucky enough to turn pro."

"Why?" Maya asked. She was genuinely interested.

"Because the conservative world of China plus the conservative world of golf equals a Cleo I don't think I would even recognize."

Cleo walked over to the window and looked down at the ground. "See now, life would be so much easier if I could just be her."

Maya looked out the window, to a girl passing below. She was a blond Glamazon, and she was swarmed by a pack of guys all jockeying for her attention.

Maya took the girl in. "Yeah, she's beautiful," she concluded. "But between the makeup, the hair, and the clothes, it doesn't look all that easy. It actually looks like a full-time job."

Maya turned back to Cleo. "I like what you've got going on. Maybe, you know, if you made it big, some little girls would like it, too?"

Cleo looked at Maya. And beamed. "I'll tell you what . . ."

"Maya," she told her.

"I'll tell you what, Maya," Cleo continued, making her first actual effort to give Maya her side of the room. "If you get bounced out of the Academy, I'm going to come hunt you down and hurt you. Because after eight months, I think I've finally found someone not ridiculous here."

Maya smiled wide, because the truth was, she'd finally found a friend, too. And, for the moment, anyway, Maya was happy to feel a little less alone.

Maya was never so grateful to take a shower in her life. She didn't think to pack toiletries (it would be the first of many things she would realize she didn't bring), so thank God Cleo was a sharer. Maya never knew so many bath products could be made from hemp. As she lathered up with bodywash and rinsed out the shampoo, she hoped she wouldn't spend the rest of her day battling the munchies.

In her hemp towel (thanks again, Cleo!), Maya made the walk from the showers at one end of the floor to her room. She turned the knob only to find the door was locked. Maya knocked. When Cleo didn't answer, she knocked again. "Cleo?" Still nothing.

Then Maya read the memo board on the door. BE BACK. *Be back? Be back from where, be back when?* Maya didn't have her key—wouldn't Cleo have double-checked that? As the reality of the situation was sinking in, Maya started to panic. *Maybe that memo was old*, she thought. Maybe it had been there when she arrived; maybe Cleo was just sitting inside polishing her golf clubs while rocking out on her iPod. Maya pounded on the door. "Cleo!" She pounded some more as denial gave way to even more panic.

"Some people are trying to sleep." The voice came from behind her. And it belonged to a guy.

Maya turned to face him as he came out of the room across the hall. From the hair to the clothes, everything about him looked like he'd just rolled out of bed. A sexy bed, but a bed nonetheless.

Maya clutched her towel closed in a death grip. "I thought this was a girls' floor?!"

"It is." He shut the door behind him. "I was just . . . visiting." And lingering. It only made Maya's face redder than it already was.

"I locked myself out," she said through her embarrassment. Stating the obvious was preferable to a silence that was getting more agonizing by the second.

"That sucks," he replied. And with that, he walked off. *That's it? No "let me call someone," no nothing?*

"Gee," she said as she stood there dripping wet and alone. "Thanks for the sympathy."

Maya began sizing up her options. It didn't take long before she realized she had none. As she looked around, waiting for any of the other girls on her floor to arrive back from class or practice, all she could think of was that famous nightmare of showing up naked the first day of school.

Suddenly, Maya heard the sound of glass breaking. It was coming from inside her room.

The door opened. To the sexy bed-head guy. "How did you . . . ?" Maya asked. She quickly made her way inside to find her window in a million pieces on the floor.

"I climbed the tree outside your window and broke in." He was awfully pleased. Actually, so was Maya.

"Thank you . . . ," Maya said, waiting for his name.

"Jake," he said. He flipped around the dog tag on a chain around his neck. His name was engraved on one side.

"Thank you, Jake," she said, still holding her towel closed. "I appreciate you doing that for me."

"I didn't do it for you," he said. "I did it because I hate this place. Any chance to break something around here, I'm taking it."

Maya couldn't have heard that right. *Because he hates this place . . . ?*

As if to prove it, Jake swiped a flowerpot off the windowsill, sending it plummeting to the ground, where it exploded like a dirt bomb.

"How can you hate the Academy?" she asked. He was already smelling like a jerk, but the sentiment was especially off-putting. "This place is a dream come true."

"Obviously you're new." He smiled. "Just give it some time." The condescension reeked.

"I don't need to give it time," she shot back. "You know how lucky you have to be to get in here?" She could feel herself getting worked up, which was so not Maya.

"*Lucky,*" he scoffed. "That's one word for it."

"If you don't like it here," she said as she grabbed a blanket and wrapped herself in it, "why don't you just leave? There are a ton of kids who'd kill for your spot. Who kill for your spot every year."

"For some people," he said, "leaving is harder than getting in. Hopefully you never have to figure that out."

Was this kid for real? All that was missing was the leather jacket and the pack of cigs tucked under his T-shirt sleeve.

"Okay," she said, at a total loss for words. "Thanks and everything."

"Well, now wait," he said. "Your roommate isn't around; there's all this crazy sexual tension between you and me. . . ."

" 'Crazy sexual'?" Maya repeated.

"Maybe we should . . . ?" He raised his eyebrows.

After way too long, what he was saying finally sank in. "What?" Maya said. "No!"

"We could just make out a little," he said. "You know, payment for services rendered . . . ?"

"Out!" She bunched her blanket around her even more, shepherding him out of the room. "Good-bye. Good-bye."

He walked out, a big smirk on his face.

"See you around, newbie," he said as he made his way down the hall. "Oh, and I know you're watching me walk away."

She was.

"I am not!" she called after him.

"Okay." She couldn't see it, but she could feel the self-satisfied smile plastered across his face.

"I'm not!" she yelled louder. He just kept walking.

Maya ran to her window and waited for him to appear down below. Finally, he did.

"I'm not!"

He just tossed her a wave over his shoulder. Her fits of denial continued as he walked away. She was officially a lunatic. She never got this angry—the guy had obviously been sent by the devil.

Maya cracked open her suitcase to unpack, but all she could think was: *what a jerk.*

Chapter 3

The bad news was that Maya's first full day at the Academy kicked off not on a tennis court but in a classroom. The worse news was that it was history, Maya's trickiest subject. She'd have to concentrate. That proved impossible with Cleo in class with her. Whenever Cleo got bored (which, judging by the loudly ticking clock planted above the door, was every thirty seconds), she would text Maya from behind her book. The texts covered a wide variety of topics, but they usually involved some form of the expression *Kill me now.*

"I'm starving," Cleo said when the bell finally, mercifully rang. "I need to get to the dining hall before I pass out."

"I haven't been to the dining hall yet," Maya said, equally famished.

"No?" Cleo asked with a smile. "Better bring a cup."

Maya thought, *Bring a cup? How does a dining hall not have cups?*

The place was packed. And even though kids were scattered far and wide with seemingly little rhyme or reason, there was something vaguely deliberate about it all. Like random herds of animals grouped together, ready to strike.

"There are written rules at the Academy," Cleo said conspiratorially. "But there are even more unwritten rules, and a whole dumpload of them exist in the dining hall." As Cleo walked them through the food line, she made sure they didn't look like they were sizing up the area. But Cleo had a bead on everyone and everything.

"Kids divide up by nationality first and foremost," Cleo said. "Sad but true. When you're thousands of miles from home, most people look for anything that's even remotely familiar. Survival 101."

Maya looked around. "How do you know who's from where?" She could pick out the Americans by the number of baseball caps and the loudness of their voices, but beyond that, she was useless.

"After you're here long enough, it'll become second nature," Cleo said, loading her tray with ketchup packets to drown the scrambled eggs that made up her entire meal. "You will be able to pick a Russian from a Belarusian from a Czech at a hundred yards in three seconds flat. Facial features, skin color, clothing, hairstyles. You'll be an international detective." Trays full, they cut through the tables en route to their seats.

"In the meantime," Cleo said, "just check their bags. The Academy is where anything with a flag goes to die." Sure enough, on closer inspection, each kid was marked by his or her own tribal colors.

"Next they're broken down by sport. Golfers sit with golfers, basketball players sit with basketball players, tiddledywinks players sit with tiddledywinks players. . . ."

"So kids do sit with other kids who play their sport?" Maya asked. "But just not if they're from other countries?"

"No, you give preference to kids from your country," Cleo corrected. "But if no one's around, you sit with your sport."

"But if there's someone from your country, you pick them over your sport?" Maya thought she had it.

"Unless you've got money. Then you sit with other rich kids," Cleo said. "Cash trumps everything."

Maya was lost, and she was happy staying lost.

"Give it time," Cleo said. "What you need to learn immediately is the Golden Rule of the Academy."

"Ooh, I know this one," Maya said. The Golden Rule was etched in stone on a giant sculpture in the middle of the quad. "*Start by doing what's necessary,*" she recited, "*then what's possible, and suddenly you are doing the impossible.*" She loved that quote.

"Please, that's just garbage they wheel out for the parents," Cleo said. "The Golden Rule at the Academy is 'Watch your back.' Everyone is in competition, even when you don't think you're in competition. Everyone has to have the best body, everyone has to have the newest Apple thingy, everyone has to have the hottest boyfriend. You are your accessories."

"I don't remember that from the welcome packet," Maya said, taking a bite from her bagel.

"Not to mention sponsors and agents are everywhere," Cleo continued, undeterred. "They're looking for the next big thing twenty-four-seven so you can never be off guard for a minute. The way you chew your food could cost you a million-dollar-endorsement deal." Maya laughed. Cleo didn't. Maya stopped midchew, suddenly wondering if there was a chance she was not doing it right and had just blown a cool million.

Just then, a charge filled the room. Maya felt it immediately. It was like a wave of magnetic energy had spread like a cloud through the dining hall. Everyone shifted his or her attention to one spot. The dining hall quickly filled with commotion, and Maya and now Cleo were looking around to see what was causing it. As kids started heading outside, it became clear that was where the action was. Maya and Cleo looked at each other, then followed the wave.

There it was, in the middle of a small mob forming. Or rather, there she was, pulling into the parking lot in a brand-new Aston Martin One-77.

It was Nicole King.

There was a lot at the Academy Maya didn't know about. But Nicole King? Nicole she knew. She was one of the main reasons Maya had fought so hard to get into the Academy. Nicole was her idol. And she researched her voraciously. A Latina from Los Angeles, she was rich, she was sexy, and she was as close to royalty as you could get at the Academy. And that included actual royalty. At seventeen, she was already a top-ten-ranked tennis superstar, known as much for the sheer power of her shots as for the sheer power of her will. She could crush a tennis ball with pure brute strength, but it was the psychological warfare she employed to win that was her greatest weapon.

And Nicole always won. Where everyone else at the Academy was scratching and clawing to go, Nicole was already there. She had the trophies, she had the million-dollar endorsements, she had the magazine covers.

"You want to close your mouth?" Cleo asked as Maya watched Nicole step out of her car. "You look like you're unhinging your jaw to eat her."

"No, it's just the car. I . . . I'm a big fan of automotive . . . stuff." But Maya rolled her own eyes at the lie.

She heard two girls whispering next to her. The grapevine moved fast at the Academy, and everyone already knew that Nicole's Aston Martin was a toy she'd bought on a whim with the prize money she'd won at her last tournament. The girls didn't seem surprised. Nouveau riche, Nicole was apparently known to blow her money as soon as she got it. Since she never lost, it was *never* a problem. Maya could only imagine what that was like.

Nicole barely noticed the crowd as she walked through with the chosen few who were allowed into her inner circle. Maya would do anything to be in that inner circle. She'd do anything just to meet Nicole.

For now, she'd have to settle for the rest of her bagel. And being really careful with how she chewed it.

Maya was in heaven. Twenty-four hours after stepping off that bus, she was finally standing on an actual Academy tennis court. Whoever said all courts were created equal had a head injury, because this was equal to nothing. It was pure magic carpet. Fresh paint, flawless bounce, a net so pristine you could swaddle a baby in it. And there were twenty of these perfect courts nearby, all full of athletes.

As she waited for her coach, she wondered what her first lesson at the Academy would be. How to hit a nasty kick serve? A sidespin drop shot? A booming inside-out forehand? Whatever it was, she was ready.

When she saw a coach make his way over, she moved to greet him. From his leathery skin, it was clear he spent every waking moment under the scorching Florida sun.

"I am so excited—" It was all Maya was able to say before the guy was screaming in her face.

"Let's go!"

Wow, he was even more excited than she was. Until she realized he wasn't talking to her. He was talking to everyone on all the courts.

"You've got thirty seconds. I want to see you lined up right here!"

He pointed to the baseline, which quickly filled up with kids. So much for Maya's private lesson.

"Today I'm gonna teach you the most important thing in all of tennis," he said, more drill sergeant than instructor. "Five simple words that will dictate the rest of your lives, at the Academy and beyond: you eat what you kill."

Maya scrunched her face. What was she killing and why was she eating it?

"Unlike team sports," he barked, "tennis players are lone wolves out there. We don't have five-year contracts. We don't get a paycheck the first of every month. What we earn each week is dictated by who we beat. You don't beat, you don't eat."

He took a racket from one of the kids. "What's this, three years old?"

The kid nodded.

"You know," he said, spinning it, "there's a brand-new model in the Academy pro shop that gives you more power and control."

"It's three hundred bucks," the kid said.

"What if I told you there was a one-thousand-dollar store credit waiting there for you to buy whatever you want?"

The kid nearly drooled. "That would be awesome."

"Well, there is," the coach said. "There's a thousand-dollar credit for all of you. Well, not all of you. One of you. Enough to buy the newest, most expensive racket . . ." He handed the kid back his antique and walked past a guy with torn-up sneakers. "New shoes . . ." He kept walking, then lingered at Maya. He looked her up and down. "New clothes."

Maya flushed. She didn't need a coach to tell her she looked like crap; she knew. And she knew what she could buy with that thousand dollars.

"All you need to do," the coach said, "is be the first person to knock this down." He took out a tiny cone, walked to the other side of the court, and placed it on the far corner of the baseline.

Without hesitation, all the kids pushed and shoved their way toward the cone. Before Maya knew what was happening, she was dead last.

"You need to hit it with a tweener." Silence. It was like a bomb dropped on the crowd.

A tweener was a ball you hit between your legs while running away from the net. Maya knew that because every time she'd tried one, she'd nailed herself in the kneecaps. Her last tweener bruise had been shaped like Africa.

"Here we go!" The coach fed the first ball, a deep lob that the first kid had to run to the back of the court to catch up with. He swung . . . and missed. The coach fed a ball to the next girl, who missed, too. More swings, more misses. The longer Maya waited, the more she thought about that money. She could buy a new everything with it. Finally, it was her turn.

She chased after the ball, swung . . . and missed.

The rotation started again. Again, it was one miss after the next. It was hard enough to hit a tweener, but to make it land in just the right spot was impossible. Maya went again. And missed.

With every miss, the tension increased exponentially. Whoever won was going to have insane bragging rights. They all wanted the kill and they wanted it bad.

Maya went again. She chased the ball. And hit the tweener! No bruise! But when the ball landed on the other side, it missed the cone by five feet. Maya wanted to scream.

"What's this?"

Everyone turned.

Nicole.

A hush fell.

"Knock the cone over with a tweener," the coach said, "and get a grand credit at the pro shop."

Nicole narrowed her eyes on the cone. "Let me borrow that," she said to the kid with the three-year-old racket. He handed it to her.

The coach fed her a deep high ball. Nicole ran for it, hit the tweener . . . and nailed the cone. *One try.*

"We have a winner!" the coach said, retrieving the cone.

The other kids were both gutted and in total awe.

"I already get my rackets and clothes paid for," Nicole said. "A store credit is worthless to me. Tell you what, I'll give it to whoever washes and details my car."

A wild offer, made more wild by the kids who all leaped at it. Maya didn't beg, mostly because if she was going to be friends with Nicole (which clearly had to happen), she couldn't be spit-shining her wheels. It was a sacrifice she felt in her gut as a lucky girl got the thousand dollars and the privilege of washing Nicole King's car.

Still, Maya wanted to hurl herself at Nicole, tell her what an amazing job she did and, oh, PS, profess her love. But there were too many kids between them. In an instant, Nicole was gone. As the other kids went back to their courts to keep practicing, Maya vowed two things: to master that trick shot and to be ready the next time Nicole came her way.

A quick break, and Maya was back on the court. With no coach to feed her balls, she was forced to bust out the big guns. Well, one big gun. A ball machine.

Maya had only hit with a ball machine a few times. It was a luxury back home, so it was wheeled out only on special occasions. Even then, it was the guy at the club who set it up. Maya knew somewhere deep down that it wasn't overly complicated, which made the fact that she couldn't figure it out that much more maddening.

Florida was two things: scorching hot and witheringly humid. Maya was already dripping with sweat after ten minutes of trying to turn the stupid machine on. Finally it kicked in, but getting it to launch balls with the right kind of spin, speed, and angle required a PhD.

As she loaded balls and watched them shoot out everywhere but where she wanted them, she caught sight of something that froze her where she stood.

Travis Reed.

Travis was standing by the fence. Out of his football uniform and in an Academy T-shirt and shorts, he looked no less immortal. As she watched him chat with a couple of kids, she couldn't think of anything else besides just how full-on gorgeous he was.

And how absolutely sweaty and gross she was.

Maya immediately dropped to a crouch behind the whirring ball machine before he could see her. When he didn't walk on right away, she desperately grabbed her cell from her pocket and called Cleo.

"Hello?" Cleo answered.

"He's here," Maya said, trying to keep her stage whisper from becoming a roller-coaster scream.

"Who?"

"Travis," Maya said urgently, ready for Cleo to freak out with her.

Cleo was unimpressed. "So?"

"So?" Maya couldn't believe her ears. "I'm talking about Travis Reed, Nails Reed's son? I told you, I met him yesterday.

I'm even grosser than I was then. What if he sees me?" Maya sneaked a look around the ball machine. He was still there, chatting away.

"Would he even remember you?" Maya wasn't sure if Cleo was simply thoughtless or if she was actually trying to punch Maya in the gut.

"Well," Maya said, ignoring her wounded pride, "if he didn't remember me, he would now." Maya scanned the area for quick exits, but the only way off the court was past Travis.

"Maya, come on," Cleo said. "How gross could you possibly be?"

Maya couldn't even begin to describe which breed of wet dog she most resembled. She pointed her cell phone at herself, took a picture, then sent it to Cleo.

"Wow," Cleo said finally. "You are gross."

Before Maya could be truly offended, she saw something that knocked every single thought out of her head.

Travis Reed took off his shirt.

Maya wasn't a boy-crazy gawker, but this guy's body was ridiculous. He wasn't a hulk (quarterbacks rarely were), but he had muscles, and they were so defined they looked painted on. By God.

"Maya?" Cleo asked. "Maya, I asked you a question."

Maya snapped back to reality. How long had she been gone?

"He just . . . shirt. Off. Body. Wow." Maya's grasp of the English language was slipping by the second.

"Did you just get out of prison?" Cleo asked, laughing. "Don't they have boys in the cornfields where you grew up?"

"Of course they have boys," she said. "And they weren't cornfields. I just . . ."

"That good, huh?" Cleo asked, intrigued. "I'd much rather see a picture of that than your unfortunate sweat stains."

"Okay." Maya raised herself just enough to get a clear shot, then covertly aimed her phone at Travis. She steadied it and focused on . . . Travis looking over at her.

Panicked, she dropped the phone without a second's hesitation. *Into the whirring ball machine.*

Please, Maya thought, *please don't let him have seen that.*

He looked away, oblivious. Maya wasn't particularly religious, but in that moment, she knew there was a higher power, and it was watching over her.

Suddenly, the ball machine clanked. Maya shifted just in time to see her cell phone launch like a rocket. It bulleted past her, through the trees, and into the nearby parking lot, where it connected with something with a loud *bang.*

Forgetting Travis, Maya raced to the parking lot. She saw her mangled phone on the ground . . . beside a car with a large dent in its side. It was an Aston Martin One-77.

And, Nicole was at the outdoor café fifty feet away from it. Nicole's walk was steady and purposeful as she made her way through the gathering crowd to inspect the damage.

"Whose is this?" Nicole asked as she picked up what was left of the phone. "I said, whose is this?"

Maya went pale. There was no way out of this. She fought her urge to run away screaming, unstuck her hair from her sweaty face, then stepped forward.

"Mine," she said. "I am so sorry." Before Maya knew it,

words started pouring out of her mouth. "It was a total accident, my phone fell in the ball machine and . . . and I know the car is new and . . . and it represents your big win at the tournament you just came from and, and that's so important, it's so important to treat yourself after a job well done, and it was, it was a job well done, and . . ."

Nicole eyed her. If Maya hadn't felt like a freak before, she definitely did now.

"What's the big deal?" Nicole said. "I'll just win another one next week." It wasn't an insult. It wasn't a joke. It wasn't even a brag. It was the truth.

"Sure," Maya said, easing. "Of course you will. I mean, you're Nicole King. I'm—" Maya stepped forward to introduce herself, but before she could finish the sentence, Nicole simply handed the phone to someone else and walked off. Along the way, Nicole joined up with a couple members of her elite inner circle, Travis among them.

Maya was left sputtering.

Travis had witnessed her humiliation, which was a nightmare in and of itself. But even more scarring was what had gone down between her and Nicole. Maya was nothing more than a flea to Nicole, not even worth handing the phone back to directly. As the intermediary handed over the corpse of her cell and the crowd they had drawn started to disperse, Maya couldn't decide what was worse: making a horrible impression on her idol or making no impression at all.

Chapter 4

Maya hated surprises. When she was seven, her father dressed up as Santa Claus, and she dropped him with a punch to the groin. Since then, it was a pretty well-established understanding in the Hart household that Maya always needed advance warning.

For this reason, Maya challenged herself to a late-evening run around the entire campus. She wanted to familiarize herself with everything. Little did she know "everything" was at least a half-marathon. Sure, she'd researched the campus exhaustively online, but she had to pound the pavement, not just her keyboard, to really know it.

As impressive as the Academy was during the day, at night it was something else entirely. The palm trees were decorated with little white lights that twinkled in the gentle, warm breeze. The fountains trickled in the quiet. But if she listened hard enough, she could hear the distant sounds of music spilling out of dorm-room windows and bursts of laughter punctuating the calm.

Exhausted, Maya cut through the Administration building on her way back to her dorm. Outside the main office, she saw a familiar face. One she almost didn't recognize without her entourage.

Nicole.

Nicole was lingering outside the locked office door.

Maya couldn't backtrack. Not because that would be running away (the urge to run and hide was becoming second nature here), but because she'd have to go all the way around the building, and her legs would not stay attached long enough to pull that off. So she pushed forward.

She had no idea what kind of greeting she'd get from Nicole, if any. So she was downright floored when Nicole turned and not only recognized her, but actually brightened upon seeing her.

"You," Nicole said, smiling.

"Nicole," Maya said, seizing the opportunity to grovel. "I am so sorry about what happened earl—"

"Yeah, yeah, yeah," Nicole said. "If you could do me a huge favor, we can call the car thing square."

Now Maya brightened. "Really? Yeah, sure. Of course." Maya could only imagine what she could possibly do for Nicole King. Give her a kidney? Give her an alibi? Whatever it was, she'd do it.

"See that framed poster in there?" Nicole pointed to a large action shot of herself on the court, ripping a vicious backhand. The look on her face was sheer brutality, a marked contrast to what Maya was seeing standing right next to her now.

"Yeah . . . ?" Maya replied.

"I was supposed to sign it for a sick kid in the hospital," Nicole said. "But this stupid photo shoot I was doing went over and I got here too late. I feel horrible. Have you ever let a sick kid down before?"

"No," Maya said.

"Me neither," Nicole said. "Because it isn't done. Not unless you're a monster or you're trying to win a bet on how fast you can spend eternity in hell. But here's the thing. See that window above the door?" It was cracked open for ventilation. "Someone tall enough could just slide through and get it. I don't have the inches, but you do."

This was about her height? The thing that Maya had been so self-conscious about was going to come to Nicole's rescue? She didn't care how tired her legs were; Maya couldn't jump fast enough.

"I can try," Maya said.

"Please," Nicole said. "Eternity is a long time."

Maya nodded, then started her climb. She was determined to pull this off. And it turned out that pulling herself up took no effort at all. Still, she'd try to sell the effort to score extra brownie points. A few more groans and a fake splinter should do it. Finally, Maya landed on the other side of the locked door.

"Yes!" Nicole beamed.

Maya grabbed the framed poster and slid it, and herself, back out.

36

"Thank you so much," Nicole said. "You have saved my soul. And maybe made a little kid's day."

Maya was glowing. "It was the least I could do." She sucked on her fake splinter.

"Well, see you around." Nicole said. *See you around.* The words echoed in Maya's head like a church bell, over and over. Nicole King will see her around. It couldn't get any better than this.

"See you around," Maya agreed.

Maya was newly supercharged, as if she'd chugged a Red Bull. She waved, then ran the rest of the way back to her place, on cloud nine.

Maya awoke the next morning at seven on the dot. As her eyes focused, they found someone standing over her bed. But it wasn't Cleo. It was an Academy security guard. Stone-faced and severe, he looked more like an undertaker.

"Maya Hart?" His voice struck like a steel baton.

"Yeah," she squeaked out. She looked around for Cleo. She'd already left for class. Being alone with this guy freaked her out even more. "What's going on?"

"Come with me, please." It wasn't a request.

Maya had five minutes to get dressed and drag a tooth-brush across her mouth before the security guard led her off. As she made her way through the quad with no idea where she was being taken or why, she felt like a criminal.

When the security guard led her into the Administration building, she saw Nails sitting outside his office. *Please don't let him be waiting for me, please don't let him be waiting for me.*

"Ms. Hart, I didn't think I'd be seeing you again so soon."

Maya's heart was in her throat as the two of them were left alone.

"Is something wrong?" Maya asked sheepishly. Something was definitely not right.

"That depends," he replied. "Do you think breaking and entering is wrong?"

" 'Breaking and entering'?" Maya gauged him. Was this a trick question?

"And theft," he added. "Did you think the security camera outside this office was there for decoration?"

Suddenly the realization flooded her.

"I didn't break anything," she said quickly. "I slid in. And I didn't steal anything; it was for a good cause."

"A good cause?" Nails asked.

Finally, Maya relaxed. Nails just didn't know about the sick kid. It made sense; he had so much to do on campus that random acts of charity probably weren't high on his radar. This was easily explained.

"There's a sick kid at the hospital," Maya said. "He was getting that poster of Nicole King, but she got here too late to sign it for him." Maya smiled. She still had time to go back and catch another hour of sleep before class.

"I have no idea what you're talking about," Nails said. "That framed poster wasn't going to any sick kid; it was framed to be hung at the Academy."

"No," Maya said. "That's not true. If it is, then someone in the office screwed up because that's not what they told Nicole. . . ."

"No one in the office screwed up," he said. "Nicole was told exactly what we were going to do with that poster, and I know that for a fact because I told her myself."

"But . . . she told me . . ." Maya paused. "She lied to me?" Maya asked finally. "Why would she lie?"

"Because," Nails told her, "Nicole didn't like how she looked in the picture. Ego makes people do bad things."

So did hero-worship. Maya felt like the biggest idiot on the planet. "What are you going to do to her?"

"She didn't break in," he said. "You did."

Maya gulped in a breath. "Yeah, but she got me to do it." Nails was unmoved. "So what happens to Nicole?" She could tell by the look on his face. He had absolutely no punishment planned for Nicole.

"Sneaking in was her idea!" Maya was getting more and more frustrated. "If you have me on a security camera, then you have her, too. You know I'm not lying."

"Nicole's put in the hard yards here at the Academy," he said. "You've been here a day and a half. She has goodwill in the bank." It was clear that Nicole's preferential treatment had nothing to do with *goodwill* in the bank. Nicole was a star and Maya wasn't, plain as that. And the realization that they were held to different rules sucked.

"The only one who actually broke a rule was you," he said. "The punishment for that is an automatic revoke of scholarship. And dismissal from the Academy."

Maya's blood went cold. "This can't be happening. I haven't even unpacked my bags yet. . . ." But she'd been caught on camera breaking into the office. There was nothing to argue about.

"Dad," a guy's voice said.

Startled, Maya turned to see someone sitting on a nearby desk. It was Travis. He'd overheard the whole thing. "She wouldn't be the first person to be duped by Nicole."

Maya didn't think it was possible, but this great big bag of crazy just got crazier. Not only was Travis Reed there, but he was actually sticking up for her?

"It's more of a rite of passage," Travis went on, playing with a stapler. "And it's not like she knew she was doing something wrong. Only Nicole did."

He was! He was sticking up for her. And he was throwing Nicole under the bus to do it. Maya wasn't sure what she'd done to deserve this, but she was not about to question it.

Maya looked to Nails. She could see on his face that his son's words carried weight. But how much? Finally, Nails rose and looked down at her. No one should ever experience this man at this angle, she thought.

"You get one warning," he said. "This was it." With that, Nails went inside his office and shut the door.

Maya let out a breath she didn't realize she was holding.

She was alone with Travis. In the cosmic balance of things, this (major) misunderstanding was totally worth it.

"Thank you so much," Maya said. "I owe you." She was more than happy to be indebted to him. To tell their grandchildren how she repaid his benevolence with a soft kiss under Niagara Falls. Well, not under Niagara—they'd drown. Under another falls. Was there another falls? And why would they be kissing under it? Maya wanted to slap herself out of whatever cycle of insanity was going on in her head. *Focus!*

"Nah, it was nothing," he said. In truth, it actually was nothing. But to Maya it was the heroic act of a knight in shining armor. He had slain the dragon in her honor.

"I'm Maya," she said. "I don't think we've been formally introduced." *Formally introduced? Who says that?*

"I'm Travis," he said.

"Oh, I know," she said. Could she sound like a bigger stalker? "I mean, your dad told me. When we saw you."

"When you . . . ?" He didn't remember her. Not from her tour with Nails, and by the looks of it, not from her parking-lot humiliation yesterday. She didn't love being that forgettable, but if that meant she had a clean slate with him, she'd take it. Happily.

"It doesn't matter," she said. "Do you make it a habit of hanging around places waiting for the opportunity to save damsels in distress?" Maya heard herself ask the question. She realized then and there that she was flirting, something she never did. And now she knew why. She was abominable at it.

"Ha, no," he said.

Silence.

Maya felt her time was running out. He didn't remember her twice and now she was in danger of being forgotten again. Three strikes and she'd surely be out.

"So . . . you just like offices, or . . . ?" She was officially grasping.

"Nah." He rolled up his track pants to tighten his laces. His calves were thick. "I'm just here waiting for my brother. We run in the morning."

"You have a brother?" Maya asked. How did she not know that?

Suddenly, his brother arrived. And she recognized him on the spot. The dog tag, the bed-head, the sour face. It was Jake.

Jake saw her. And laughed. "Wow. I heard someone broke into the office last night. It was you?"

Maya was shocked. That miserable dude was a Reed? The kid who hated the Academy so much he'd take any excuse to smash something here? He was Nails's son? Travis's brother?

"You two know each other?" Travis asked.

"No," Maya said, just as Jake said "Yes."

"She probably doesn't remember me," Jake said. "Because she was staring at my behind the whole time."

Maya went blank, except for three words: *Oh, my,* and *God.*

"Gotta run," Jake smirked by way of a good-bye, then pulled Travis out the door.

Maya was left behind to wrap her mind around what had just happened. And wonder what on earth Jake could possibly be whispering about her in Travis's ear right now.

Oh yeah. Maya hated surprises.

Chapter 5

"What are the chances?" Maya walked through the quad with Cleo and repeated the only words she could get out. "What are the chances?"

"I don't get it," Cleo said. "How did you even meet Jake in the first place?"

"He broke me into our room when I got locked out," Maya said, her head still spinning.

"That's who broke our window?" Cleo asked. "Why am I just hearing this detail?"

"I wanted to bleach my brain of the whole experience," Maya said, queasy at the mere memory of it. "He was awful. I was stuck out in the hall, and he came slithering out of some girl's room—"

"Which room?" Cleo asked quickly.

"The one across the hall," Maya replied.

"I knew it!" Cleo said. "I knew that girl was a skank!"

"Not really the point of the story," Maya said.

"Right, sorry," Cleo said. "She is a skank, though."

Maya pressed on. "All he kept saying was how much he hated the Academy. When he wasn't trying to hook up with me, that is. I can't believe how different he and Travis are! Jake is a spoiled jerk, and Travis saved my life. I've been killing myself to make some kind of impression on Travis. I can't even imagine what Jake has told him about me!"

"Wait, back up," Cleo said. "Travis saved your life? How?"

"I almost broke your record for shortest-lasting roommate," Maya said. "I was crazy close to being kicked out if it wasn't for Travis. Actually I *was* kicked out when he got Nails to change his mind."

"Kicked out?" Cleo asked, wide-eyed. "For what?"

Maya was too embarrassed to tell her, but Cleo wasn't going to let her off the hook.

"I ran into Nicole King outside the main office last night," Maya said finally. "There was this poster of her that I guess she thought she looked terrible in. She tricked me into breaking into the office to steal it for her."

Cleo started to ask a question, but Maya stopped her.

"Because I was an idiot," Maya said. "That's why. I'm lucky Travis was there to plead my case or else I'd be on the bus home right now."

"What happened to Nicole?" Cleo asked.

Maya shrugged. "Nothing. Technically she didn't do anything wrong."

"What do you mean, she didn't do anything wrong?" Cleo asked.

"She stayed outside while I did the actual deed," Maya told her.

"I don't get it," Cleo said. "If what you did was bad enough for you to get kicked out, it was bad enough to get her kicked out."

"I'm just telling you what Nails Reed told me," Maya said. "She had 'goodwill in the bank' or something."

"Unbelievable!" Cleo said, steamed. "Nicole King could get some girl to break into an office and steal something for her and get away without a slap on the wrist, but you needed his son to keep you from getting your whole head chopped off!"

"Cleo, calm down," Maya said. An angry Cleo was a scary Cleo.

"No," Cleo said. "You should be getting more angry. This is ridiculous."

"I know, but come on. . . ." Maya motioned around them. They were getting looks.

"There are different rules for different people here, and I'm sick of it!" Cleo closed her eyes and breathed deep, calming herself down. "Nicole can't get away with this," she said simply. "If the Academy won't make her pay, we will."

" 'Make her pay . . .'?" Maya asked nervously.

Cleo grinned. "We're going to strike where Nicole will feel it the most."

As intimidating as Nicole was, Maya still couldn't help but fear for her in the face of Cleo's fury. And also fear for herself.

Cleo and Maya made their way from the quad to the practice courts. On court one, Nicole was swinging away. It was one thing to see Nicole strike the ball on TV, but in person it was something else. The power was staggering. Every time Nicole hit the ball, it was as if Maya could feel the force of the blow. How did she get that good? Maya wanted to know. Badly.

She also wanted to know what Cleo had in mind for Nicole, which was still just as big a mystery.

"Listen," Maya said. "I don't know what's going on in that mind of yours, but I've hit my trouble quota. I've already gotten kicked out of the Academy once today."

"Relax," Cleo said. "We're not going to get in trouble."

Nicole hit her last serve, then returned her racket to her bag. She quickly toweled off, threw her bag over her shoulder, then left.

"Too late," Maya said, relieved. "She's gone."

"And we're going with her." Cleo smiled.

Cleo watched as Nicole headed into the locker room. Then she grabbed Maya's arm and followed.

By the time Cleo and Maya arrived inside the locker room, Nicole was already in the shower. Visions of *Psycho* danced in Maya's head, and she hoped there was nothing sharp and pointy nearby.

Cleo's eyes searched, then landed on Nicole's tennis bag. "There it is," she whispered. She went over to it, unzipped it slowly to keep the noise down, and then started digging maniacally.

"What are you doing?" Maya said in a hushed yell. Cleo didn't stop. "She could come out of the shower any second and see you in her bag! Are you insane?"

Maybe Cleo *was* crazy. Had Maya aligned herself with a lunatic?

Cleo just stayed focused on the task at hand. Finally, she located what she was searching for and pulled it out. Nicole's cell phone.

Maya was even more confused—and more freaked out—than before.

"It's unlocked," Cleo said, pleased. "Really, Nicole, for someone sooo famous, you should protect your stuff better."

As Maya watched, totally rooted to where she stood, Cleo took Nicole's phone and tiptoed closer to the shower. Maya went bug-eyed when Cleo proceeded to slip it under the shower door—and take a picture.

"Cleo!" Maya hissed.

Cleo just smiled and scurried back. She held the picture out to Maya.

"How awful is this?" Cleo asked giddily.

Maya looked at it. The picture was totally harmless, revealing nothing. But between her tangled, wet mess of hair; the contorted look on her face; and the epically awkward angle of the shot, it was without a doubt the single most unflattering picture of Nicole Maya had ever seen. Actually, it was the single most unflattering picture of anyone she'd ever seen.

"Awful," Maya agreed. "Can we go now?"

"We're not done," Cleo told her, having fun.

Maya had had enough.

"Okay, that's it," Maya said. "What is this plan? Tell me now."

"Okay," Cleo said, relenting. "Nicole's always on Twitter and Facebook."

"I know," Maya said. "I follow her on foursquare, too."

Cleo rolled her eyes. "And assuming she doesn't log in and out with every single stupid thought she's compelled to share with the world . . ." Cleo confirmed her theory as Nicole's Twitter account popped right up on the screen. "Nicole wanted to keep that framed poster out of sight because she didn't like how she looked in it. Well, then, we're going to hang a worse one. For everyone to see."

Cleo handed Maya the phone, the picture attached and ready to go out on Nicole's Twitter feed.

Maya went wide-eyed. "We can't do that!"

"You're right—*we* can't," Cleo said. "You were the one who was wronged. You should get the honor of pulling the trigger."

"No, no, I can't," Maya balked.

"We have to do this," Cleo asserted. "Maya, these rich kids can't get away with treating scholarship kids like we're gum on the bottoms of their high-heeled shoes."

"Yeah, but this picture . . . ," Maya said. She looked at it again. It was truly awful.

"This picture is barely even PG," Cleo said.

"Listen, Cleo, I get what you're saying," Maya said. "But . . . Nicole is my idol. Yeah, she did something crappy, but it's not like she did what she did to get me in trouble."

"Exactly," Cleo said. "She used you just to use you."

Maya's face was suddenly hot. And it wasn't from the steam.

"She set you up with absolutely no care in the world about what it would do to you," Cleo continued. "And while you were getting kicked out, you know what she was doing? Sleeping like a baby."

Maya was getting even more heated.

"Your idol, Nicole King, stopped thinking about you the minute you were out of sight," Cleo said. "You weren't even worth a second thought. How does that feel?"

Almost despite herself, Maya's thumb flinched. It was just enough to press the send button. In a flash, the photo went out into the universe. In an even faster flash, Maya immediately regretted it.

"Oh my God," Maya said.

"Oh my God," Cleo repeated.

Maya stared at the phone in her hand, her thoughts racing. What did she just do?

"Now what?" Maya asked in a panic.

Just then, the phone jumped in Maya's hand. The vibration of a call, combined with a ring. Texts started pouring in, one after the other. *Beep. Beep. Beep.*

The cell storm was loud. So loud that the water in the shower immediately turned off.

Cleo smiled. "Now we run."

They tossed Nicole's phone back in her bag and raced off as fast as their legs could carry them.

Maya and Cleo were at the Underground, a late-night campus hot spot filled with pool tables, leather couches, and a bar that served everything but alcohol (which just turned half the kids there into smugglers). Neither Maya nor Cleo was dying to go out, but Nicole's Twitpic had spread like wildfire, and Cleo thought it was best they hide in plain sight. Guilty people wouldn't go out in public, right?

"Everyone's staring at us," Maya said at the bar, sipping her Coke.

"You always think people are staring at you," Cleo said. It was amazing how quickly Cleo had gotten to know Maya, and how accurately.

"This morning was a warning," Maya said. "That's what Nails Reed told me. If anyone finds out I sent that picture . . ."

Cleo shushed her.

"If anyone found out," Maya said in a tone so hushed even she herself could barely hear it, "I'll be done. Gone. Everyone is talking about this. Even the teachers, the coaches . . ."

"That was the point," Cleo said. "It was supposed to be a big pie in the face. And she had it coming."

Suddenly, something changed. The air in the room took on a static charge. People shifted. Maya and Cleo looked at each other. They had felt this once before.

Nicole walked in.

"Oh God," Maya said.

"Wipe that look off your face this second," Cleo said. "You might as well spray-paint *guilty* across your forehead."

Maya altered her face. She altered it again. She couldn't get it to feel natural.

Cleo looked at her blankly. "Now you just look crazy."

Maya studied Nicole as she made her way through the crowd. You'd never think she'd suffered a split end, much less total and utter humiliation. She was, in fact, quite calm. She was cool. She was . . . coming their way?

Maya looked to Cleo, sat bolt upright, and sucked on that straw like it was her job.

"Just relax," Cleo warned her. "If you say or do something to implicate us, I'm giving you up, I swear."

"I'm a terrible liar," Maya said. "My face is full of tells. I can't think up anything on the spot. . . . My face is twitching. Can you see it? It's totally twitching."

"Maya! Get a hold of yourself!" Cleo said without moving her lips.

Finally, Nicole reached them. Maya had sucked down an entire Coke in five seconds, but her mouth was still bone-dry.

"Iced tea," Nicole said.

Maya allowed herself to relax. Nicole wasn't beelining to them, she was beelining to the bar.

"If you want to pull pranks on people," Nicole said, lazily pouring sugar into her iced tea without so much as turning around, "you should probably do it somewhere without so many mirrors. Or learn to run faster."

Maya choked on her ice cube. Finally, the dam that was her mouth burst.

"I am so sorry," Maya said. "That was just . . . awful, and I'm awful, and if I could take it back I would, in a second, in half a second!" Maya was coming apart at the seams.

"You know," Cleo said to Nicole. "You were the one who scammed Maya and got her kicked out."

Maya didn't want to incite Nicole, even if it was with the truth.

"Yeah, but I got un-kicked out, so no harm, no foul. Please don't rat me out," Maya begged. "I'll be bounced for good."

For the first time, Nicole King turned around. Her expression revealed nothing. And that terrified Maya. If Maya's face was full of tells, Nicole's was as illegible as they came.

Finally, Nicole spoke. "You're right. I had it coming."

Maya was stopped. "What?"

"It was a crappy thing I did," Nicole said as her expression lost all severity. "I didn't think of how it would affect you, and I'm sorry. So, we're even."

"Actually," Cleo pointed out, "technically Maya's one up on you thanks to the whole car thing."

Maya elbowed Cleo. Hard.

"Thank you," Maya told Nicole. She was overcome with an inexplicable urge to curtsy. She thought better of it.

"I'll just tell everyone I posted that pic myself," Nicole said. "I did it on purpose to . . ." She thought for a moment, but just a moment. "To inspire people to embrace their flaws."

That was brilliant, Maya thought.

"Of course," Nicole continued, "if either of you tell anyone you did it, I'm going to look like a big liar, so you can't say anything. To anyone."

"No, no, of course not," Maya agreed enthusiastically. "You got it, we won't tell a soul."

Not only had she evaded retribution, she might have even turned a corner with Nicole. Maya shared a secret with her idol. This could be the beginning of a beautiful friendship.

"Besides," Nicole said, "I don't want to be known as the girl who got a couple of scholarship kids kicked out."

With that, Nicole walked off.

Cleo rolled her eyes. "Please," she said the minute Nicole was out of earshot. "She wasn't being nice; she just doesn't want anyone to know she got punked. And by lowly scholarship kids! This was a PR move, nothing more. She's good. But whatever, we're not getting in trouble. That's all that matters."

For Maya, it wasn't all that mattered. She was left even more depressed than if Nicole *had* ratted them out. Because this proved she was an even bigger nothing at the Academy than she'd thought. To Nicole and to everyone.

Chapter 6

Maya sat on the quad feeling sorry for herself. Cleo was running late, so she had plenty of time to wallow in her own suckitude.

Maya wasn't an idiot. She didn't think coming to the Academy would be a big slumber party where everyone would stay up late doing one another's hair and putting one another's underwear in the freezer (at least that was what she'd heard happened at slumber parties—she'd never actually been to one). She didn't expect to feel so alone, though.

She had Cleo, and thank God for that. But that didn't make her feel any more like she belonged. Of course, that was not what she'd told her mother on the phone that morning. The sun never shined brighter and the air never smelled sweeter if you believed what Maya had spewed to her. If Maya couldn't manage her own emotions, at least she could manage her mother's.

Just then, on the grass in front of her, Maya saw something truly bizarre. It was a blond Glamazon poking around the grass like a flamingo. Upon closer inspection, Maya saw that it wasn't just any blond Glamazon. It was Nicole King's roommate! In Maya's near-pathological attempt to learn everything about her idol's life on campus, she'd discovered that Nicole didn't live alone. There were a couple of girls who had the money, power, and looks to be worthy of sharing a private on-campus villa with her. Renee Ledecq was one of those girls.

Maya figured out that Renee was painstakingly searching for a lost contact. Turns out no amount of money, power, or looks could save you when you were blind. Maya studied her, but, thanks to Cleo, she was already an expert about this girl she'd never met.

She knew Renee was aloof and unapproachable. She was part French, part South African, and 100 percent filthy rich. Unlike Nicole, who at least earned her money, Renee got hers completely from her parents. Her father was an ambassador (to what country, Cleo had no idea, much less what an ambassador actually did), and her mother was a socialite (which Cleo had assumed was code for a raging alcoholic with money).

According to Cleo, Renee was also perhaps the most hated girl on campus. Not because she always had the nicest stuff (though that didn't help), nor was it because she vapidly threw her money at anything and everything (again, not a plus). What made her a legend among the girls was that she was a legend among the guys. Renee always had a guy on each arm, and it was never the same one twice. Word around the Academy was that she was the easiest score on campus.

As Maya continued watching Renee, Renee turned from a flamingo into a dog, sniffing around on her hands and knees. And getting more panicked. What started out as entertaining morphed into downright painful to watch.

"Do you need some help?" Maya dared to ask.

"Please," Renee said. When Renee finally looked up, Maya could see why she was so desperate. Those perfect, big blue eyes of hers were actually colored lenses—and one was missing.

"I can't see a thing without my contacts," she said. "If I can't find my other lens, I'll have no choice but to walk around with one in and look like a total freak, and I . . . I can't handle that."

Although Maya didn't totally get the tragedy of it all, she felt Renee's anguish. So she sniffed around with Renee. Finally, Maya spotted a spec of blue among the green.

"Got it," Maya said, picking it up carefully.

As Maya handed it over, the relief that came over Renee was palpable. She pulled out a bottle of contact solution, gave the lens a quick wash, and popped it back in her eye.

"I owe you one," Renee said. A lot of owing went on at the Academy, Maya thought, but if there was one person you'd want owing you, it was Renee.

"What's your name?"

Maya was struck by the question. Not because it was an unnatural next step, but because it was the first time anyone had actually asked. Until now, she was the one who had had to offer it.

"Maya," she said.

Renee smiled. "I love that name. I'm Renee."

Maya marveled at her accent for the first time. It was

amazing. It was a combination of French, South African, and something else Maya couldn't place. The result was Renee speaking like no one she'd ever heard in her life, even on TV.

"Where are you from?" Renee asked.

That was also the first follow-up question Maya had received. Usually, whoever she was speaking to had taken off by then.

"Syracuse," Maya replied. "It's in New York. The state, not the city."

"I've never been. What's it like?" Renee asked.

This wasn't the girl Maya had heard so much about. This Renee asked questions and seemed genuinely interested in the answers. Was Maya the one getting punked now?

"Um, it's cool," Maya said. Then she thought about it. "Actually, it's not cool. It snows thirteen months a year and the only thing to do on a Friday night is go to the supermarket. And people, like, look forward to it."

Renee laughed. "You're a riot."

"Oh," Maya said, "if you think stories about working-class people are funny, you'll think I'm hilarious." Maya was seeing just how far she could push it with Renee. Renee only laughed more. There was no judgment; she was simply entertained.

"You're new," Renee said.

"Do I have a sign on me?" Maya wanted to fit in, not stand out. She feared what signals she was giving off.

"You're talking to me," Renee said.

Maya wasn't sure what to think. "People must talk to you all the time," she said.

"Guys," Renee said. "Guys talk to me all the time. Girls

don't want any part of me. They think I'm stupid, or I'm going to steal their boyfriends, or buy their boyfriends—I don't know."

By the look on her face, Maya could see that Renee really didn't know. And it seemed to bother her.

"Or they know I don't belong here," Renee said finally.

"Why wouldn't you belong here?" Maya asked. She had just met this girl, but she already had this overwhelming sense of . . . something for her. It felt a lot like sympathy.

"Because my parents bought my way in," Renee said. "They didn't want to deal with me at home, so they shipped me off."

"From what I've been able to tell so far," Maya said, "you're not the only one who paid your way in."

"Yeah, but the difference is I suck," she said.

"I'm sure you don't suck," Maya said.

"No, I suck," Renee maintained. It wasn't in a self-deprecating way. She was just being . . . honest. "I'm a swimmer. Quote unquote. It's a wonder I don't drown the minute I dive in."

Maya couldn't even imagine being here in the middle of all this hypercompetition and not be any good. It must've been like being invisible.

"I don't want to suck," Renee continued. "I want to be great. Maybe then my parents will want me around."

Maya felt guilty. More than guilty. She had bought into what she'd heard about Renee and had written her off because of it. But Renee wasn't aloof or unapproachable at all. She was beyond nice, and beyond open. Maybe she was just too intimidating to strike up a conversation with. Or maybe people here just didn't care about conversation at all. Regardless, Maya had believed what she was told again, and again it wasn't true. She vowed that was the last time she would make that mistake.

Just then, Cleo arrived.

"Cleo, hey," Maya said, then made introductions. "Cleo, Renee. Renee, Cleo."

As Cleo smiled through clenched teeth at Renee, the look Cleo gave Maya said it all; of every girl on campus, why on earth was she talking to this one?

"We were going to hit up the dining hall," Maya told Renee. "Do you want to come with?"

Cleo shot Maya another look. Maya avoided her eyes this time.

"Oh, the dining hall?" Renee scrunched her face. "That's not good enough to eat at."

"Ah," Cleo said quickly. "Maybe next time."

"No," Renee said, "I mean I want to take you out to a better lunch. For finding my eye."

"I found her contact," Maya said to Cleo. "Hey, free lunch!" Maya poured on the enthusiasm with Cleo, fully aware her roommate did not want to spend any more time with Renee. "How can you say no to that, huh? Huh?"

Maya would not be denied. Cleo glared at Maya with such intensity it could've burned a hole through her brain.

Renee didn't do anything small, and lunch was no exception. They were at a table at a five-star restaurant just outside campus. There was a fireplace that took up a whole wall, an impressive mural on the ceiling, and a view of the ocean so spectacular it looked CGI. It was the first time Maya had been off campus since she got here, and she felt free. Being here, she felt like a royal.

Cleo looked like she was caught in a bear trap and was fully capable of gnawing her foot off.

"What's the spending limit?" Maya asked jokingly. As soon as she said it, she feared that Renee would think she was serious and ban her from the kingdom.

Renee laughed. "The limit is your belt. The minute it pops, you're done. Just because I can't eat doesn't mean you can't."

"Do you have a disease?" Cleo asked. It was less a question and more of a stab. Maya caught it; Renee didn't.

"Yeah, it's called fat," Renee said, searching the menu.

"'Fat'?" Maya asked. She and Cleo shared a look. Renee was a size four on her worst day, and that was while wearing a parka.

"Fat for me," Renee said. "You can't be the daughter of an ambassador and look like Ursula the sea witch. That's what my mother says, anyway."

"Yeah," Cleo said. "But if you just want to roll out of bed and grab a doughnut somewhere, you can do it, right?"

"Roll out of bed, like, leave the villa without doing my hair or makeup?" Renee raised her eyebrows.

"Are you serious?" Cleo asked. The conversation seemed to be luring Cleo into actually paying attention.

"You're lucky," Renee said. "You don't look like it, but you're both pretty."

"Wow," Cleo said sarcastically. "Thanks."

"No, I mean you don't have to do all this extra work." Renee motioned to herself. "I do. People expect it. Guys expect it. Do you think they hang around me because they want to know all my hopes and dreams? They hang around me because I look this way. They think I'm special. And the thrill they get when they hook up with me, well . . . that gives me a thrill, too. But I'm still all made up like a drag queen."

The more Maya listened to Renee, the clearer it became that her self-esteem was completely out of whack.

"It does catch up to you," Renee said finally. "At the Academy, it's just . . . the pressure to measure up is so intense, in every way. One slipup and you're toast. Gossip flies faster than any ball here, and the second people can hang you, they will. It's just . . . it's just hard."

Maya could tell Cleo was now having the same moment she'd had earlier. Cleo was starting to sort of like Renee. And it was pissing her off.

"I have a crush," Maya said. She was inspired by Renee's sharing and wanted to do a little of her own. "On a guy named Travis."

"Travis Reed?" Renee asked. "I'm friends with him."

Maya's face turned red. Of course they were friends. Nicole was friends with him, and Renee was Nicole's roommate. How could Maya do something so thoughtless?

Renee read her mind. "Don't worry about it. I won't tell anyone, I swear."

Maya believed her. "He's just so . . . God, and his face . . ." Maya lost all ability to string words together where that guy was concerned.

Cleo mock-wiped drool from Maya's chin.

"Tell me he's nice," Maya begged Renee. "That he rescues kittens from trees and volunteers to read to the blind while on breaks at the soup kitchen."

Renee chuckled. "He's cool," she said. "He's smart, and pretty grounded for someone who walks on water."

"Would he date a scholarship kid?" Maya asked, feeling like her life depended on the answer.

"I've never seen him with one," Renee said. Maya's face fell. "But he's not a huge dater. He's pretty focused on his future. He's being groomed for something big."

Maya brightened. She could work with that.

"Jake, on the other hand." Renee shook her head. "If you were looking to hook up with a Reed and you were on a deadline, he's your guy."

"Yeah," Maya said, "I've already been gifted the request. That would not give me a thrill."

"It might give you a disease," Cleo said, and laughed. Maya and Renee joined in. With the three of them laughing together, the Academy was a million miles away.

"Come on, Cleo," Renee said, leaning in with a devilish look in her eye. "We're sharing secrets. What's yours?"

Renee looked at her, waiting for her to give it up. Maya knew better.

"Cleo's not really a secret-sharer—" Maya began.

"I kissed a girl," Cleo said, interrupting.

Maya looked at her, shocked. Cleo seemed to be shocked she'd said it, too. Where did that come from?

"When?" Maya asked.

"The night before you got here," Cleo said. In the short time she'd known Cleo, her roommate had been closed up tighter than a vault, but something about the conversation made her dare to share.

"That was only a few days ago," Maya said. "Was that your first time?"

Cleo nodded.

"Is that why you've been so edgy?" Maya asked.

"No," Cleo said. "I'm always like this."

Maya nodded. *Okay.*

"Well," Renee asked, "what did you think? Of the kiss?"

Cleo took a second to think about it. "It was . . . cool," she confessed. "I guess. I don't know what it means. I've only ever kissed guys, and I'm pretty sure I liked that, too. I'm so confused. And I'm not used to being confused. I hate it." Cleo looked to Maya and Renee. Maya could tell that, for all the bluster Cleo put out, she cared what Maya and Renee thought. She was waiting for them to say something. Anything.

"You know, you *can* question your sexuality," Maya said. "It doesn't make you weak. It certainly doesn't make you any less of a person if you did like . . . you know . . ." Maya stumbled over the words.

"Are you having a stroke?" Cleo asked.

"I'd support you no matter what," Maya said, unwavering.

"Me too," Renee said.

Cleo tensed. This kind of unabashed sentiment seemed to be too much for her. Maya needed to cut the tension, fast.

"You know what?" Maya said, leaning into Cleo. "Forget everything I said about Travis. I'm over him. I want you now." Maya grabbed Cleo and tried to kiss her on the lips.

"What are you doing?" Cleo yelled, and flailed back.

"Oh yeah, me too," Renee said, playing along.

"Stop!" Cleo screamed, pushing them away. But she couldn't push away a smile. And soon a laugh.

"I'm going to throw up. Get away from me!" Cleo finally pushed them off, but they just kept laughing. "You guys are idiots." Then more quietly she said, "Thanks for the support."

"You'll be fine," Maya told her. "You just need to relax."

"And you need to gargle some mouthwash," Cleo retorted. Maya had calmed her down, for the moment, anyway.

This was turning out to be the best lunch ever.

Just then, the waiter approached.

"Good afternoon, ladies," he said. "Have you decided what you'd like?"

The girls looked at one another, surprised. All this and they hadn't even ordered yet. They didn't have to say it. The smiles that crept across their faces said it all.

Maya, Cleo, and Renee returned to campus red-faced from laughing. And very stuffed.

"I think my belt popped," Maya said. They laughed some more.

"This was so much fun, you guys," Renee said. "I don't have a lot of girlfriends here. If it's not too cheesy, I kind of wouldn't, you know, mind it . . ."

"All right, fine," Cleo said. "Stop begging. You're embarrassing yourself. We'll be your friends."

Maya's friendship went without saying.

Renee beamed. "Okay, good. Now you have to come to my party."

"What party?" Maya asked.

"I'm having a big costume party at the villa this weekend," Renee told them. "Everyone will be there."

"The villa, like, Nicole's villa?" Maya asked.

"Well, me and another girl pay the rent there, too," Renee said. "Or at least our parents do."

Maya looked at Cleo, both of them fully aware that Maya hadn't told Renee about her bizarrely frequent run-ins with Nicole. Maya didn't want to stir up any trouble. She couldn't decide if Nicole's being at the party was a good thing or a bad thing.

"Travis will be there, too," Renee added with a grin. *She did not play fair.*

"You know," Cleo said, "I don't know if I'm comfortable being at a party with a bunch of rich kids. No offense."

Renee nodded.

"Come on, Cleo," Maya said, swooping in before the final verdict was rendered. "One drink couldn't hurt, could it?"

Cleo eyed her. "Are you really going to force me to go? For Travis?"

Maya's face was unmistakable. *Why, yes. Yes, I am.*

Chapter 7

The knock on Maya and Cleo's door was important for two reasons. One, it was the first time anyone had knocked on it the entire time Maya had been at the Academy (unless you counted the handyman who came to replace the broken window, which Maya didn't). Two, it meant time was running out on a deadline Maya was dreading.

"Come in!" Cleo called.

Renee walked in, her face full of excitement and expectation. It was the evening of the costume party, and she'd come to see what Maya and Cleo were wearing. Maya watched as Renee's face fell.

Cleo was sitting cross-legged on the floor in a cheerleader's outfit, smearing black eyeliner on her face, which she'd covered in open wounds.

"What kind of a costume is that?" Renee asked.

"Isn't it obvious?" Cleo asked. "I'm a zombie cheerleader. Redundant, I know." Cleo started hacking away at her skirt with a razor. She was in hog heaven.

"Oh, Cleo," Renee said, flummoxed. "Costume parties aren't about face makeup. They're about transforming yourself into something extraordinary. Something magical. Something sexy, for God's sake."

"I think I look plenty sexy," Cleo said.

"At least you're something," Renee said, turning to Maya. "What's going on with you?"

Maya was sitting on her bed in a towel.

"I'm stuck," Maya said. "I don't have any ideas. None."

The truth was, even if she had an amazing idea, it would never be able to make its way to her brain, because all she could think about was the fact that Travis would be at the party. He would see her in this costume, and he would have an opinion.

"You're worried about Travis," Renee said. "And you want him to like whatever you're wearing."

"What are you, a mind reader?" Maya asked.

"I'm a girl," Renee said. "And you're a girl. It's biology."

"What biology class did you take?" Cleo asked.

"It doesn't matter, anyway," Maya said. "I don't have a chance with him."

"Why would you say that?" Renee asked, sitting on the bed next to her.

"Oh, I don't know," Maya said. "Maybe because he's a kajillionaire and I grew up collecting soda cans for the nickel deposits? Ooh, or maybe it's because he's the most sophisticated guy on the planet and I'm just crawling out of the woods like some kind of Appalachian hillbilly? Or maybe it's because, no matter how hard I try, no matter how much game I have on the court, I have absolutely none off of it. That's it, that's the one."

"Hey," Cleo said, getting off the floor and sitting beside Maya, too. "That is garbage. Every word of it. It doesn't matter how much money you have or don't have, or how refined you are. He's not better than you, Maya. And if he thinks that, you don't want him anyway."

Maya wasn't used to Cleo being so emotionally supportive. She was taking on this cheerleader role hard-core.

"Besides," Cleo continued, "if you don't have a chance with Travis, it's obviously because of what Jake told him about you."

Maya fell face-first onto her pillow. And screamed.

"Too mean?" Cleo asked. Maya didn't even have the strength to lift her head up and glare at her.

"You're worried about making an impression on Travis Reed?" Renee asked, throwing her a lifeline. "I'm going to make sure you make an entrance he'll never forget. You're going to go as me."

"Excuse me?" Maya asked, her face muffled by the pillow.

"Well, not as me, exactly," Renee said. "I'm not that vain. I mean all dolled up. You'll look smoking hot, and you'll get the added bonus of seeing just how much work goes into looking like this."

Maya laughed. "Smoking hot? I don't think there's enough stage makeup in the world to pull off that transformation."

Renee sized Maya up, her interest suddenly piqued by the challenge.

"We'll see about that," Renee said.

Maya could not believe she was here. She couldn't have orchestrated it if she'd tried, but somehow, inexplicably, Maya Hart was inside Nicole King's villa. She had cracked Wonka's factory.

The party was still hours away, but Renee needed those hours to prepare. She was going to transform Maya. Into what, only Renee knew. And that scared Maya. But if it meant she could finally make some kind of impression on Travis Reed, she would happily submit.

Obviously what she was submitting to was something extraordinary, because it required tools found only in Renee's laboratory. But before they could get to her bedroom, they would have to make their way through the rest of the villa. And the rest of the villa was mind-blowing.

Maya felt every bit the trespasser, and though she tried to look nonchalant, she wasn't blind. As they walked through the place, she could see it was dripping with cash. It was also massive. The furniture, Renee told her, was imported from "somewhere in Africa." It clashed "the right way" with the state-of-the-art projection system in the living room. Over the couch was a Picasso that Maya convinced herself was a fake so she wouldn't start freaking out. In the end, Maya felt she was trespassing not into someone's home, but onto a movie set.

"Nicole?" Renee called out. Maya held her breath in the silence, waiting.

"Hm, she's not home," Renee remarked.

Maya was at once relieved and disappointed.

"My room is just back here," Renee said. She led her down a hallway, past an open bedroom door.

"That's Nicole's room," Renee said.

As she walked past it, Maya craned her neck to see inside. Even if Renee hadn't told her whose room it was, Maya would've known. Maybe it was the fact that it was big enough to fit her entire family. Maybe it was the tennis bag next to the raised, hyperornate canopy bed. Or maybe it was the giant Andy Warhol–esque painting of Nicole hanging directly above it. Maya was pretty sure Warhol died before Nicole was born, so he couldn't have painted it himself, but if anyone could raise the dead to do her bidding, it would be Nicole King.

Finally, they arrived at Renee's bedroom. It was equally enormous, but what left Maya speechless was her closet. Correction, closets.

"Oh my God," Maya said, her jaw dragging on the floor. "Are these all your clothes?"

"No," Renee said. "Most of my clothes are back home. It made no sense to bring a ton of stuff, since it's only ever a hundred degrees here."

"Right," Maya said. "No sense at all."

The clock ticking, Renee led Maya into her closets and attacked them like a hurricane. There was nothing for Maya to do but gawk. Everything was separated by category. Dresses here, skirts there, shoes everywhere. There was an entire spinning rack for sunglasses, whole shelves for bags.

Maya picked up a pair of red boots from a sea of identical red boots.

"Why do you need twelve pairs of the same shoe?" Maya asked.

"What are you talking about?" Renee said. "They're all different. This one is alligator, these are crocodile, these ones are python. . . ."

"PETA is going to burn you at the stake," Maya said.

Renee stayed focused on the task at hand.

"Since this is a costume party, I can't just throw you in a dress and call it a night," Renee said, digging. "This needs to be theatrical. Lucky for you I've got something perfect. I bought it before Nicole got a brainstorm, and now she and I are going as something else."

"What's the costume?" Maya asked.

Finally, Renee found it. "It's my favorite movie character of all time. She's amazing." Renee unveiled the costume to Maya. It was a huge dress for a Southern belle on a plantation.

"Scarlett O'Hara," Renee said, beaming. The dress was red and dramatic and spectacular. It was also enormous. There's no way it would fit in Maya's closet, but Renee had plenty of space.

"Who's Scarlett O'Hara?" Maya asked.

Renee shot her a look. "Who's Scarlett O'Hara? How deep in the woods were you raised? *Gone with the Wind*?"

"I've heard of that," Maya said.

"You've 'heard' of that?" Renee said, exasperated. "I wasn't even born in this country and I've seen it. Maya, it's amazing. Scarlett O'Hara is rich, she's beautiful, and all the guys fight over her. She's also really smart. She made a gown out of curtains."

"Was it a comedy?" Maya asked.

"No, this conversation is," Renee said. "But it's about to get really serious." Renee's face suddenly had a hint of evil.

"What are you going to do to me?" Maya asked, fearful.

"What am I *not* going to do to you?" Renee grinned.

What happened next was a whirlwind. Before Maya knew it, she was sitting at a makeup mirror, a towel around her hair, and a face steamed, squeezed, and tweezed to within an inch of its life. One thing Maya did know for sure was that beauty hurt like hell.

Renee appeared to be in a state of rapture, applying paint to her blank canvas and transforming Maya into her version of a work of art.

But when Renee stopped midway through and stepped back to inspect her work, her face fell.

"What?" Maya asked.

Renee stopped doing Maya's makeup and moved on to her hair. She took off the towel, exposing the wet hair she had subtly darkened to fit the character. Again, Renee was displeased. Maya didn't like this at all. Finally, when Renee pulled the giant red dress over Maya's shoulders and stepped back, Renee groaned.

Maya couldn't take it anymore. "Okay, what?" she demanded. "What's wrong?"

"You," Renee replied.

Maya was crushed. She never put on makeup or got dressed up. Now she knew why.

"Everything about you is ridiculous," Renee went on, annoyed. "The hair, the body, the lips. I wanted to give you a makeover, but I hardly have to do anything. All I'm doing is throwing a little makeup and a twelve-G handmade dress on you. I hate you."

Maya could've registered what was an amazing compliment (though she swiftly would've shot it down) if something else hadn't taken up the entire space in her head.

"This dress cost twelve thousand dollars?!"

"Yeah," Renee said. "I got it on sale."

Maya stood there dumbfounded while Renee continued styling her.

With music booming in the background, Maya opened the villa door to an impatiently waiting Cleo.

"I've been ringing the bell forever," zombie cheerleader Cleo said. "This is how you treat the dead?" She tried to move around Maya without even acknowledging her.

"What?" Maya said, blocking her way. "Not even a comment on the outfit?"

Cleo took her first real look at her "Maya?!"

Maya laughed. Cleo burst out laughing, too.

"Oh my God, I didn't even recognize you! What did Renee do to you?" Cleo couldn't get over it. "That dress is enormous. You look like you belong on top of a cake!"

"Hold me!" Maya fell into her arms, mock-sobbing. But the tears in her eyes were real.

"I want to hug you, but I can't find you," Cleo said, fighting her way through layer after layer of red tulle.

"Fiddle-dee-dee," Maya said, wiping her tears indignantly. "I'm practicing being melodramatic. I'm Scarlett O'Hara. Apparently I'm an emotional headcase."

Cleo finally pushed Maya off her. "Well, Scarlett, I don't want to get any of my open sores on your pretty dress," she said.

"You better not," Maya said. "It cost twelve thousand dollars."

Cleo laughed. When Maya didn't, Cleo's eyes grew wide.

"Are you serious?" Cleo asked incredulously.

"She got it on sale," Maya said. "Apparently there are markdown bins with twelve-thousand-dollar ball gowns in them somewhere."

"You need to steal it and trade it for a car," Cleo told her. Maya laughed. This time it was Cleo who didn't. Maya swatted her.

"Come on," Maya said. "I hear there's a party going on in there."

"How is it?" Cleo asked.

"Couldn't tell you," Maya said. "They have a third roommate, Christine. She's the daughter of a state senator or something, but she's not around much. I've been upstairs in her bedroom waiting for my hair to set. And being made to watch *Gone with the Wind*." She reached for Cleo's hand, then affected the best Southern accent she could muster. "Shall we go inside?"

Cleo gave her pom-poms an exaggerated shake, and then they headed into the party.

Cleo was almost as awed as Maya had been upon seeing

the wonderland inside. Except this time, besides being packed with museum pieces, it was also packed to the walls with costumed revelers. Vegas showgirls and Roman emperors, Greek goddesses and Prohibition-era gangsters. From the tops of their heads to the tips of their toes, everyone looked flawless. And, as Renee had pointed out, sexy.

The party was not only in full swing, it was in full roar. People were screaming, music was blasting. There were fireworks being shot off the balcony.

"How has this party not been shut down yet?" Maya asked, removing a shot glass from a potted plant.

"Different rules for different people," Cleo said. "Or did you forget?"

They made their way through the crowd, Maya pretending to be trying to find someone when secretly she was just showing Cleo the rest of the place.

"I heard about the villa," Cleo said above the music as she tapped the glass of a wall-mounted aquarium, "but I never could've imagined this."

The tour continued. Renee was nowhere to be found, and without her to claim them, they were on their own. Strangers in a strange land. Thank God Maya and Cleo had each other.

"I need to use the bathroom," Cleo said.

"Wait, you're just going to abandon me?" Maya asked. "What am I supposed to do, talk to the fish?"

"I'll go fast," Cleo promised.

Maya looked around. "I'll wait for you on the balcony," she said, noticing that there was hardly anyone out there now that the fireworks were over.

Cleo gave her pom-poms another little shake, and then they split up.

Maya and her giant dress fought her way through three Marilyn Monroes and a Little Red Riding Hood before finally arriving outside on the balcony. She turned to take in the view. She found another one instead: Travis, right in front of her face. He was dressed as the king of clubs. A very, very sexy king of clubs.

"Travis," she said, her face heating up on the spot. "Hi."

"Hi," he said. He didn't recognize her. Again.

"It's Maya," she said. "You saved my life?" When he didn't react right away, her face got even more red. Just when she thought coming here might've been a huge mistake, another thought popped into her head. One far, far worse. What if he did recognize her . . . and just didn't care?

But then Travis's eyes narrowed. "Maya . . . ?" His jaw dropped. "You look . . . amazing."

Did Travis Reed just tell her she looked amazing?

"Your hair," he said. "And your eyes. Were they always this blue?" Maya owed Renee big-time. The plain hair and too-blue eyes Maya always felt saddled with became other-worldly in Renee's hands. Renee wasn't just a good friend—she was her fairy godmother.

"I'm Scarlett O'Hara," she said. "She made stuff out of curtains." Maya couldn't roll her eyes harder at herself. *She made stuff out of curtains? Seriously?* She had to move on immediately if not sooner. "And you're a playing card!"

"You like?" he asked.

"Oh my God, yeah," she said. "I just want to stick you in my bicycle spokes." Maya really needed to stop speaking.

Travis laughed. He actually laughed.

"Listen," Travis said. "Sorry about my dad. With the whole 'break-in' thing. He can be tough. It was nothing personal at all."

"So if I caught him on another day, he wouldn't have kicked me out?" Maya asked.

"No, he would've," Travis said. "He just might've felt a little bad about it."

Now they both laughed. For the first time, she felt like he was actually paying attention.

"Wow," she said, taking him in.

"What?" he asked.

"Just . . . you talking about your dad and everything. I can't get over how similar you two are," Maya said. "I mean, duh, you're father and son, but . . . it's not just your looks. It's your mannerisms—it's even how you stand." Maya hoped she was making sense, but she couldn't trust anything coming out of her mouth at this moment.

Travis lit up. Whatever she'd said was the perfect thing to say.

Just then, Julius Caesar popped his head out.

"Travis, emergency in the kitchen, dude," he said.

Maya's heart sank. This was it? But they were just getting started!

Travis started to go, then turned back to her. "Maybe we can pick this up somewhere quieter?"

"Somewhere . . . ?" Was he asking her what she thought he was asking her?

"Do you know where Christine's bedroom is? Upstairs?" he asked.

She'd only spent the last two hours there. "I think so," she said.

"Maybe I'll see you up there in a few minutes?" Travis didn't move. He was waiting for her answer. As if there was more than one answer to that question.

"Sure," she said quickly. "I mean, yeah, maybe. But sure."

He smiled. "Great."

With that, Travis went inside. It was Maya's turn to beam. And take one seriously long, deep breath. Okay, breathing done. Now she needed to find Cleo.

Maya left the balcony. As her eyes searched for the only dead cheerleader there, she wound up running straight into the queen of hearts. It was Nicole. She was with Renee, the queen of diamonds. If decks of cards were this hot, people might still play with them.

"There you are," Renee said. "I've been looking all over for you!"

"Hey," Maya said. "Great party."

"It is great, right?" Renee asked with a huge grin.

"Great," Maya repeated. She already lacked social graces, but being around Nicole, especially after everything that had gone down between them, had her more tongue-tied than when she had been on the balcony with Travis.

Renee turned to Nicole. "I don't know if you know my friend Maya. . . ." Maya looked at Nicole like a deer in headlights. What would Nicole say to her? What would she do? Finally, Nicole spoke.

"Nice dress, Maya," Nicole said pleasantly. Then she motioned for Renee and walked on. Renee followed, gesturing to Maya that she'd be back.

Maya's brain went into overdrive. Had Nicole not recognized her all made up? Was she being polite because Maya was friends with Renee? Ultimately, Maya didn't care. Nicole King had called her by her name and complimented her dress!

Maya's cleavage vibrated. She pulled out the cell phone she'd tucked away in there. She'd replaced the last one with a refurbished one, using the credit card her father had given her "for emergencies only." If not having a phone wasn't an emergency, she didn't know what was.

Maya found a text from Cleo: "SAW GIRL I KISSED. PANICKED. TOOK OFF."

Maya's eyes suddenly darted everywhere. The girl Cleo kissed was here? Which one was she? Maya was dying to know. More important, though, was the fact that someone, anyone, had made Cleo panic. Maya didn't think that was possible. Obviously, her friend needed her.

Then she thought of Travis. Upstairs.

It was no choice at all. She wanted to be there for Cleo. She needed to be. She decided to go upstairs, say good-bye to Travis, and leave. And pray he'd want a rain check.

Maya climbed the stairs and made her way back to Christine's room. When Maya had left it, the lights were on and *Gone with the Wind* was playing. Now everything was off. She'd gotten there before Travis.

Or so she'd thought. To her side, in the moonlight, she could just make him out. Her king of clubs, standing in the dark, waiting for her!

"Hi . . ." Her voice was barely audible.

"Hey . . . ," he said back, in a whisper that made her toes curl. Before she could stress out over what to say next, he stepped closer, took her face in his hands . . . and kissed her.

It wasn't just any kiss. It was epic. Which is why Maya, though at first surprised, gave into it. She was in this spectacular villa in this gorgeous dress, and she was kissing Travis Reed! This might just be the most amazing moment of her life. No, there was no *might* about it. This was it. This was it right here. And she wasn't going to blow it with her own cracked-out neuroses.

As they turned and stepped into the moonlight, everything Maya saw began burning into her brain. The gold threads in the seams of his sleeve, the white sash leading down his chest, the giant black spade fixed onto his shoulder . . .

Spade? That's not right. Travis was the king of clubs. Wasn't he? She shifted him full-on into the moonlight.

Jake.

Maya leaped back and threw on the lights. There was Jake, her Scarlett-red lipstick smeared across his face.

"What do you think you're doing!?" Maya fumed.

Jake was glassy-eyed. Drunk.

"Turn off the lights. Come on," Jake pleaded. "I have a splitter."

"I couldn't care less!" Maya yelled. "Are you out of your mind?!"

"Travis was pulled into an ice run," Jake said. "He sent me up here to entertain you until he came back."

Maya couldn't even blink. "This is how you entertain someone?"

"Well, that depends on you," he said. "Are you entertained?"

"No!" she huffed.

"Really?" he replied. "You seemed entertained."

"I . . . ! You . . . !" Her brain seized. "This . . . !" she stammered, fists clenched, until she finally just stormed out.

She passed Renee at the base of the stairs.

"Maya!" Renee said. "Finally, now we can hang out!"

Maya just blew past her, careening toward the door.

"Where are you going?" Renee asked.

But Maya was already gone.

Chapter 8

It was 7:30 a.m., and Maya and Cleo were still in bed. They were wide awake, but neither of them could face the day. Not now, and maybe not ever.

"I ran away," Cleo said. "Like, people say 'I ran,' but I *literally* ran. I knocked a flamenco dancer on her ass."

"What's her name?" Maya asked.

"The flamenco dancer?" Cleo asked.

"The girl you kissed," Maya said, exasperated.

"Svetlana." Cleo said it into her pillow, but Maya could speak muffled.

"Oh, Svetlana," Maya said with a sexy smirk. "She is Russian, no?"

"Please stop," Cleo said, throwing her pillow at her. "Yes, she's Russian. She runs track. And I'm pretty sure I out-clocked her last night."

"Cleo kissed a Russki," Maya sang.

"I swear to God I'll break your fingers," Cleo said.

"I'm sorry," Maya said, fighting to rein it in. "Did Svetlana see you?"

"Yes," Cleo said.

"And?" Maya asked. Cleo was twisting her bedsheet around her fingers so hard they were turning purple.

"And she smiled," Cleo said. "She smiled. I ran."

Maya wasn't used to seeing Cleo so raw. Or confused. She knew she'd have to tread delicately here or risk losing not just a finger but an entire limb.

"Well, you know . . . ," Maya said. "Maybe running wasn't the answer."

"Oh no?" Cleo asked. "How did your night end?" She raised her eyebrows at Maya.

"Okay," Maya said. "Point taken. What I'm saying is, if you're confused about . . . everything . . . maybe you should, I don't know, spend a little time with Svetlana. See how you feel."

"It's not that simple," Cleo said, sitting up. "It's complicated enough not fitting the image of a typical Chinese girl. Having a girlfriend on top of that? That would just be . . ."

"Worry about that stuff later," Maya said. "Right now you're a nobody."

"Thanks," Cleo shot back.

"Well," Maya said. "What better time to figure this out, while you're still a . . ." Maya looked at Cleo eyeing her, ready to strike. ". . . an unknown?"

Cleo breathed deep.

"So, what?" Cleo asked. "Go on a . . . date? Or something?"

"Or something," Maya said. "It doesn't have to be that serious. Just hang out. Go to the Underground. Maybe she likes playing pool . . . ?"

Cleo was quiet for a minute. "I'll consider it," she said finally. Then she looked at Maya. Though she was trying to hide it, her face gave way to an ever-so-slight appreciative smile. Maya knew not to make a big deal out of it. That'd be a good way to lose a limb.

"You're lucky," Maya said, tossing back her pillow. "Kissing a girl is a dream compared to kissing Jake Reed."

"Okay, come on," Cleo said. "How did you not know it was him?"

"It was dark!" Maya cried. "Same height, same build. They were both dressed as playing cards!"

"That's the dumbest costume I've ever heard," Cleo said. "Were bingo cards not available?"

"Focus!" Maya said.

"Okay, okay." Cleo calmed her down. "How was it? The kiss?"

Maya didn't even want to think about it.

"Horrible," Maya said. "I can still taste the alcohol on his breath." That's all she needed to get up and grab her toothbrush. She slathered on some toothpaste and began maniacally dry-brushing her teeth.

"You okay there, champ?" Cleo asked, amused.

"You know what?" Maya said through her brushing. "This was nothing. What happened to you and me last night? Not even worth remembering." She grabbed the trash basket and spit toothpaste into it like a madwoman. "There were people at that party who have a lot more to be embarrassed about. One guy, I think he was the son of a congressman, he barfed over the side of the balcony."

Cleo laughed. "You're lying."

"Nope!" Maya said as she continued brushing. "There was this second cousin of a British royal—"

"Who?" Cleo asked.

"I don't remember who. I don't follow that stuff." Maya spit, then got back to feverishly brushing. "I do remember the girl was so wasted she danced on a table for money."

"Shut up!" Cleo screamed.

"And all she got were coupons," Maya said.

Now Cleo nearly spit. "You're definitely lying. As if someone at that party had coupons."

"Ask Renee, I swear!" Maya laughed.

"Those people are hot messes!" Cleo said, wiping her eyes. They were still wet.

Maya gave up on brushing. She couldn't have gotten rid of last night's kiss any more if she gargled with bleach.

"I bet you can't wait to get out of your makeover, right?" Cleo asked.

Maya had somehow crawled out of her dress, but her makeup and hair were still camera-ready.

"Eh," Maya said. "A couple more days of this could be good for a laugh. Something we could obviously use. Now, come on, the day's a-wastin'."

Cleo hurled her pillow at Maya.

Maya grabbed Cleo's foot and forcibly dragged her out of bed, with Cleo kicking and screaming the entire way. Finally, she was on the floor.

"I hate you," Cleo said to her.

"I hate you, too." Maya smiled back.

"Yesterday really happened, didn't it?" Cleo said.

"Yes, it did."

Things got broken at the Academy. Bones, records, spirits. Tennis strings were right up there on the list. Kids hit with ferocious brutality here, which meant having a stringer with a walk-up window right by the courts wasn't just a convenience; it was a necessity.

Maya was at the window collecting one of her rackets when she spotted a woman waving her arms on a court. She was in a Prada suit. What would possess someone to wear a suit on a tennis court? And in ninety-five-degree heat, no less? The woman waved again. Maya realized she was waving at her. Confused, Maya grabbed her racket and made her way over.

As she got closer, she saw a small crowd. Then she saw someone else on the court. Nicole.

"I'm Jordan, Nicole's agent," the woman said in a British accent as stylish as she was. No hello, no "What's your name?" If possible, this woman dispensed fewer pleasantries than her client. "Nicole's hitting partner came down with a touch of something. Can you fill in?" There was a question mark at the end of that sentence, but it wasn't a request.

"Um, sure," Maya said nonchalantly. Or as nonchalantly

as she could muster. She kept her head down as she walked past some spectators and onto the court.

Nicole looked over. She was in total business mode. Obviously, it had been her idea to call Maya over, since Jordan had no way of knowing who she was, but it wasn't exactly a social call. Nicole just needed a warm body. Maya, on the other hand, just needed to make sure she didn't make a total fool of herself. Especially not in front of Nicole.

"No time for warm-up," Jordan said. "Things to do." And with that, Jordan took a call.

Maya shoved a few balls into her pocket and, with her freshly restrung racket, fed one to Nicole. Nicole returned it, clocking it past Maya like a bullet. Maya was going to have to adapt fast or this would be over before it began.

Nicole crushed the second ball, but this time Maya at least got her racket on it. Maya was able to return the third ball back to Nicole, and with the fourth ball she was able to rally. Spectators were gathering on the sidelines, and it distracted Maya enough to get pegged in the chest by a volley.

"Ow!" Maya winced, winded. Nicole held up a hand as an apology. It would've meant more if she hadn't made the gesture over her shoulder while walking back to the baseline.

If Maya was going to have any hope of hitting the balls, she needed to tune out the crowd, and her own brain chatter. She focused harder than she had on anything in her life. The rallies got longer. The crowd got larger. But Maya couldn't celebrate, because it seemed the better she did, the more vicious Nicole became.

Maya fed another ball, which Nicole hammered with purpose. Maya got it back, but that only made Nicole hit it harder to the other side of the court. Maya somehow managed to run that ball down, too, and Nicole blasted it to the opposite side of the court. Nicole had Maya on a string, but Maya was, fantastically, still holding on.

The point took on marathon proportions as it became a clash between an irresistible force and an immovable object. No one hit harder than Nicole—not just at the Academy, but in the world—which made Maya's defensive skills look positively elite. But Maya wasn't used to a single point going on this ruthlessly long, and she was running out of gas fast. Pulled so wide off the court and knowing she'd never be able to run down the next ball, she went for broke, hitting a tweener lob and sailing into the back fence. When she looked back, she saw the ball fly over Nicole . . . and touch the back corner of the baseline. If there had been a cone there, it would've gone flying. It was a clean winner.

And the crowd went nuts.

She didn't know if it was the victory or the total lack of oxygen in her brain, but Maya was suddenly flying awfully high.

Nicole, who had barely broken a sweat, simply fed another ball.

Maya's moment of triumph was followed by a million moments of humiliation as she helplessly watched ball after ball fly past for the next forty-five minutes. She didn't touch a single one of them. Maya was totally drained, and Nicole made her pay.

The crowd went from cheering for Maya to praying for her to totally giving up on her. Before she knew it, her time was up.

Maya barely had the strength to make her way to the net. She won a battle, but Nicole won the war.

"That was fun," Maya said through gasps of air. Somehow, being publicly flogged didn't make the experience any less exciting.

"Could I have set you up for that tweener any more?" Nicole asked. She was smiling, but it was that kind of smile that said she was thoroughly bothered. "I need to work on my pace," she added. "I might as well have thrown you the ball underhanded on that shot."

Here Nicole had absolutely demolished her, but all she could fixate on was the one point she'd lost. Was that what it took to be a world champion, or was Nicole just insane?

"Thanks," Jordan said, in the middle of a call. Brokering a deal for Nicole took precedence over showing any gratitude to Maya. Or eye contact.

Maya and Nicole left the court to a throng of suck-ups. There was no compliment too big to throw at Nicole. No volume too loud.

"Can I get a picture?" a photographer asked. "Not for me; I'm with the Academy."

"My agent is right over there." Nicole directed him to Jordan. "She handles everything." It was clear that even if the photographer was with the Academy, Nicole was still in charge. And she didn't work for free.

"I was talking to this girl," he said, gesturing to Maya.

Maya looked at him. So did Nicole. Their looks said the exact same thing: *Her?*

"You're beautiful," he said. "Professionally speaking, of course."

"Oh," Maya said, rather dazed. That oxygen clearly hadn't made its way back to her brain. She was sweaty. She was flushed. But she was also still sporting her makeover from last night. "Um . . . I guess?"

Waiting for him to set up his camera, Maya stood there completely taken aback. As Nicole watched, that same forced smile spread across her face. It was obvious Maya wasn't the only one in total disbelief.

As Maya made her way back to Watson, her mind was still at the courts. But not on the courts, shockingly. She'd gone toe-to-toe with Nicole King (for one point, anyway), a fantasy daydream spectacular she'd had since the first time she saw Nicole play on TV. And yet it was what had happened off the courts that had her thoughts swirling. The only things Maya had ever heard about the way she looked were how freakishly tall she was, how creepily blue her eyes were, how plain blond her hair was. Suddenly, those were all pluses? She had gotten compliments last night, but she'd attributed that to the dress and the cleavage. But today there was no twelve-thousand-dollar gown in sight, and the photographer had still wanted a picture of *her.* In addition to plucking Maya's brows, rouging her lips, and hot-oiling her hair, Renee must've chucked fairy dust on her.

"Maya!" a guy's voice came from behind her. She turned. It was Travis, running after her.

"Maya, I've been calling you since the football field."
Travis was smiling, even if he was out of breath.

"Sorry, I . . . I get lost in my brain sometimes," she said.
"It's a tricky place, lots of booby traps." Maya hadn't perfected
talking to Travis yet, but she was too distracted by the fact that
Travis was chasing after her to care.

"Sorry for last night," he said. "I got dragged away. Literally dragged. Ice emergency."

"Oh, wow," she said. "Yeah, ice melts." Okay, now she was
hearing herself. She wanted to run face-first into a pole just to
shut herself up.

"I would much rather have spent that time with you."
Travis flashed his million-dollar smile.

That urge to self-injure went right out the window. She
was flooded with goose bumps. Finally, she willed herself to
speak.

"I had to leave early," she said. "To go take care of a friend."

"That's great," Travis said. "Not that you left early or that
your friend needed help or anything, just that you put them
first. Loyalty means a lot to me. You don't find that in many
people."

Maya blushed. The way he was looking at her was intense.
Normally she'd look away or crack a joke. But this time she just
looked back. It was a completely, totally, fantastically romantic
moment.

"Travis! Maya!" Jake had a pompous grin across his face as
he threw an arm around each of them. "What a night, huh?"

Maya smelled the alcohol on his breath. "Looks like yours
is still continuing," she said.

"You know," Jake said pointedly, "you brush and you brush, but some tastes you just can't get out of your mouth."

Maya tightened up.

"I hope you weren't too annoyed with Jake last night," Travis said. "I'm used to apologizing for him, so this wouldn't be anything shocking."

Wouldn't it?

"Not at all," Maya said. "I was only with him for a few minutes before I had to go."

Jake met her eyes. Maya looked away.

"Listen, Maya," Travis said, suddenly shifting. "I wondered if you wanted to hang out tomorrow night."

"You mean, like, go-see-a-drive-in-movie-together hang out?" Was he seriously asking her out?

"Yes," Travis said. "Like a drive-in-movie date."

Oh my God, he is seriously asking me out.

"I don't know when the last date you went on was," Jake said, interrupting the moment, "but they haven't had drive-ins since *Grease*."

Maya ignored Jake. "That would be . . . great."

"No maybe?" Travis asked.

"No, no maybe." She smiled.

"Pick you up at six, then," he said. "Okay, I've got to get back to the field before someone jacks all my stuff. See you later!" He smiled (*that smile!*), then ran back.

Maya stood there basking in this moment. Jake just stood there.

"You didn't tell him about kissing me," Jake said.

"You kissed me," she retorted.

Jake shrugged. "Semantics. You covered it up for a reason. If I didn't know any better, I'd say it was because you liked it so much."

"You don't know any better," she said.

"Then I'm right." He smiled, triumphant.

"What? No!" She was getting louder.

"Well, now you're getting flustered." He wouldn't let up. "Look how red you're turning." Jake was harder to rally against than Nicole.

"I'm getting red because you're making me flustered!"

"There's nothing wrong with enjoying a kiss between friends," he said.

"It wasn't a kiss between friends!" Maya was pretty sure she was now full-on maroon.

"I notice you didn't argue with the enjoyed part," he said, smiling. "See? I knew you liked it."

He walked off.

"I didn't like it," she called after him. "I didn't like it!!"

Why did every conversation with Jake end with her screaming after him like a lunatic?

Maya steadied herself. She had far, far more important things to worry about.

She had a date.

Chapter 9

Renee sat on Maya's bed applying eye shadow. Unlike at the costume party, where Maya was basically her mannequin, Maya had to pay attention. At some point, she was going to have to do something called "reapplying," and apparently that was an area rife with pitfalls.

"First you apply a dark shade along your lash line," Renee instructed her. "Then you put a medium shade on the crease, like this . . . and then you put a light shade up to the eyebrow bone but not beyond. Then you want to blend any hard edges so it looks like one color is melting into the next."

Maya was already lost. She glanced at Cleo, who was using an eyeliner pencil to black out a tooth. "Don't look at me; this is your bright idea."

Maya turned back to Renee. "You do this every day?"

"No, of course not," Renee said. "This is obviously for a nighttime look. I do something totally different for daytime."

She brushed out Maya's hair. "Your hair's actually held up pretty well from the other night."

"Figured," Cleo said. "It had enough hair spray in it to choke a horse."

"Look who's making fun," Renee said. "How long did your hairdo take?" Cleo's hair had gone from red to blue, with purple tips.

"This isn't vanity," Cleo said. "I'm expressing my individuality."

"If it takes you two hours to do it, it's vanity." Renee smiled. Then, finishing Maya's hair and makeup, she unveiled the pièce de résistance: a stunning blue Vivienne Westwood cocktail dress.

"Holy . . ." was all Cleo could say.

Maya was equally blown away. "If this dress cost anywhere near twelve thousand dollars, I don't want to hear it."

"Twelve thousand! Ha!" The way Renee said it opened up the very real possibility that it had cost a hell of a lot more.

Maya put the dress on. Wearing it, she felt like she was visiting another planet. But it wasn't an entirely unpleasant trip.

"Good God, Maya," Renee said, shaking her head. "With those legs, that cocktail dress is now a micromini."

"I'll wear something else," Maya said.

"No, it's hot," Renee said. "The ball gown was a costume; this . . . this is just you. I'm getting that feeling of hatred for you again. It's really not fair."

Maya still had no idea how to take a compliment. Any she'd received in the past were for her on-court play, and she could say thanks and mean it because she worked hard for that. But getting compliments on something she had no hand in? How do you say thanks for that?

"What do you say or do on a date with the millionaire son of a sports icon and the Academy owner?" Maya asked.

"It's no different than a regular date," Renee said, fixing Maya's bra straps.

"Okay, that doesn't help," Maya said. This is where Renee could really make fun of her. If Renee were that kind of girl.

"It's like a game," Renee said. "You like games, right? Well, this is a game you play in a cute dress and heels."

Okay. Maya was listening.

"The object of the game," Renee said, "is to make the guy feel like he's winning the entire time, but in the end, you've got them by the you-know-whats."

"How do you do that?" Maya asked.

"With your girly charm," Renee said.

Maya stared at her blankly.

"You build them up," Renee said. "You make them feel attractive and manly. You open your mouth and lick your lips. You laugh at his jokes. You compliment his masculinity. What he doesn't realize is that he's playing by your rules. You're controlling the game. He gets addicted to feeling that good, and to keep getting that fix, he'll do whatever you want. Game over. You win."

Maya was unsure. "Open my mouth . . . ?"

Renee was exasperated. "Okay, look. I'll be the girl, Cleo will be the guy."

Cleo put down the eyelash curler she was using to pick

crumbs off her shirt and keyed back into the conversation. "The minute I tell you I kissed a girl, I have to be a guy?"

"Just play along," Renee said. She sauntered over to Cleo, who still had her blackened tooth. "So, what are you doing there?" Renee asked seductively.

Cleo just eyed her. "Looking for escape routes?" Renee swatted her. "Okay, okay. Uh . . . greasing up my hog."

Maya looked at Cleo. "Greasing up your hog?"

"If I'm going to be a guy, I'm going to be the hairy-chested, knuckle-dragging gorilla kind," Cleo said. She mock-spit into her hand, wiped it clean on her jeans, and shook Renee's hand. Renee was undeterred.

"Ow, you almost broke my hand. Such a strong hand-shake," Renee purred. "I like strong hands." Renee licked her lips. Maya couldn't decide if this was a valuable lesson or a trainwreck. But she wasn't looking away.

"That ain't all I got that's strong," Cleo said. It didn't make sense. But it didn't have to. Renee laughed anyway as if it were the funniest joke she'd ever heard in her entire life and before.

"You're bad." Renee slid closer to Cleo. "My mother would kill me if she knew I was talking to a bad boy like you."

Cleo couldn't help but grin.

"You like bad boys?" Cleo asked, getting into it.

"Maybe," Renee cooed. "I really like when people have the guts to do what they want and just say screw it, you know? Screw what people think. Like, shaving half their head . . ." Suddenly, Renee snapped out of it, caught off guard by Cleo's hair. "That's actually a really great cut, Cleo. Where did you get it done?"

"I did it myself," Cleo said, thrown to be yanked out of their role-play.

"You're lying," Renee said. "You shouldn't be a golfer; you should be a hairstylist."

"No." Cleo waved her off.

"I'm serious!" Renee kept studying it. "I pay a guy in Paris a fortune to cut my hair, and you do it better than he does."

Cleo blushed. "Really? Wow."

Renee looked to Maya and smiled. "See? All it takes are a few compliments and they're eating out of your hand."

Cleo and Maya both gaped. Renee had just played Cleo, and she'd completely fallen for it.

"Wow," Maya marveled. "That's evil."

"It's not evil," Renee said. "It's being a woman. See, not so silly after all."

"How did you learn all this?" Maya asked.

"You can't grow up around my mother and not pick up a few tips." Renee swept her makeup into her bag.

Suddenly, a car honked just down below. Renee went to the window. Travis was sitting in his glossy white Mercedes Roadster convertible.

"Your chariot awaits!" Renee said.

Maya poked her head out to confirm she wasn't dreaming.

The restaurant was amazing. It was more like an oasis than a place to eat. On the water, it was open-air with long, flowing white curtains that blew gently inside, tea lights on every table, and more flowers than you'd find at a presidential funeral. Maya would've been aware of all of this if she could take her eyes off the menu for one second. But they were fixed to it like glue. Focusing on the pretty writing was so much easier than focusing on the pretty guy sitting directly across from her.

"This place used to be a Taco Bell until Justin Timberlake bought it," Travis said. He seemed as relaxed as she was wound up. "Now you need a headshot and a résumé just to get a reservation."

"Mm," Maya said. She was too engrossed in her menu to be able to elaborate on that. Or so she would've had it appear.

"Do you know what you want?" he asked.

She'd been staring at the menu for the better part of twenty minutes, but she was no closer to knowing what she wanted to order. She didn't recognize half the ingredients. What was agri-doux? And did she want it with mousseline or jus? And even if she could figure out what this stuff was, she'd never be able to pronounce it. She should've known she was in trouble when she saw that no prices were listed.

"Um," Maya said finally. "Maybe you could order for me? I trust you."

Travis smiled. "Cool." Her utter helplessness masqueraded nicely as a show of faith.

When the waiter arrived, Travis ordered something for the both of them that he told her would change her life. She would've been more excited if ordering hadn't meant the waiter taking her menu.

"You look really nice tonight," Travis said. "That dress. And those shoes—those shoes are intense. You're as tall as I am now."

She smiled. Under the table, she slid one shoe off and

massaged the blood back into her foot. Maya had worn heels a few times, so she could almost walk in them without looking like she was trying to navigate a bouncy castle, but they were still and always would be torture devices.

"Renee says you're from New York," he said. "Manhattan, Brooklyn . . . ?"

Maya gulped. She knew where this line of questioning was going. At some point it was going to lead to the boonies, all the hick things she did growing up, and what her parents did to pay the bills. Her father didn't run an Academy; he ran a landscaping business, and he ran it out of the kitchen. He didn't own a small city; he owned four secondhand lawn mowers, a beat-up pickup truck, and a signed photo of Travis's father. If she wanted a shot at a second date, she needed to avoid this topic like the plague.

"New York, New York, the town so nice they named it twice," she said. Wow, she thought, even for her that was abominable. She tried to save it. "But Miami! Only one name for Miami. Because it's so amazing. Miami, Miami. See, that wouldn't even make sense. Miami period. That's the business. That's the stuff." Maya's mouth was quicksand. The more she struggled, the faster she sank. She needed to do something fast or this whole night was not only ending in disaster, it was ending before the food arrived. Since she clearly couldn't trust her instincts, she decided she had no choice but to trust someone else's.

She opened her mouth. And licked her lips.

"Are you okay?" Travis asked.

"Why do you ask?" She licked her lips again.

"Uh . . . no reason," he said. He studied her for a second and then just continued the conversation. "So you're a tennis player. It's so weird, trying to get a ball from one side of a field to another is everything to me—it makes all the sense in the world. But, no offense, getting one over a three-foot-high net does absolutely nothing for me."

Maya laughed. Way too hard.

"That's so funny," she said. "I never thought of it like that. You're clever. I guess you'd have to be to be a quarterback."

"Um. Yeah, I guess. You're sort of the strategy guy." Travis buttered a roll. "The mental part of the game is what I love. Unlike my brother, who just mauls people."

"He's . . . something," Maya said.

Travis was smart. Smart enough to pick up on what Maya was thinking.

"You don't like him," he said.

"I wouldn't say that." Maya wondered how she could change the subject from Jake back to New York, New York.

"Because you're too nice," Travis said. "But I know he's a jerk."

Maya contorted her face, less to protest than to conceal how thrilled she was that Travis saw Jake was a jerk, too.

"Don't get me wrong," Travis said quickly. "I love him and all that. He's my brother. But he's worse than a third grader sometimes. I try to stick up for him, but it gets harder and harder the more ways he finds to embarrass himself. And my family. Since my mom's not around, he's just gotten worse."

The waiter came and refilled their water glasses. Travis didn't continue until the guy was out of earshot.

"Sorry, you can never be too careful," Travis said. Maya wondered if that was one of the quirks of being born famous. "Where was I?"

"Your mom," Maya prompted.

"Yeah, well. She's in Hamburg or Prague or Milan or who knows." Maya could see the subject of his mother was not an easy one to talk about. "Bumming around Europe on the never-ending vacation. She keeps saying she'll be back next week or the week after. It's been months. Meanwhile, my dad's parenting solo. He and Jake are oil and water and . . . oof.

"I know he's saddled with me as a brother. My dad likes me more—everybody likes me more. I don't lord that over his head, but that doesn't stop other people from doing it. It's a lot to live up to. But I work hard, and I'm grateful for what I've got and I take advantage of it. Jake just pisses and moans. He doesn't even like football; he just plays so he can rage out on other guys."

Maya laughed again. But again, that wasn't a joke.

The waiter arrived with their first course. He placed two plates in front of them, then moved on.

"I hope you like mussels," Travis said.

"I can't help but notice your muscles," she said.

He didn't respond. He didn't need to for her to know she was going down in flames.

"Look," he said finally, leaning in. "Obviously tonight was a mistake."

Maya's heart buckled.

"You live in Watson," he said. "You obviously didn't grow up with what I grew up with. Even this restaurant is making you nervous." She couldn't speak. This was it. "How about I take you someplace where we can just take it easy?"

Maya lit up. Oh thank God, he wasn't dumping her on the spot.

"That would be great," she said.

"Cool," he said. "I had something else in mind anyway."

Travis dropped cash on the table and walked Maya out.

After waiting for the valet, they got back in his car. It was a beautiful night, and as the wind blew through Maya's hair, she prayed she wouldn't humiliate herself any further on this date.

Finally, Travis pulled into a parking lot.

And that's all it was. A crappy parking lot in an abandoned warehouse district. He cut the engine and the headlights, and they sat in the dark.

Maya was suddenly flooded with the realization of what was really going on here. Of what Travis had in mind. She was humiliated. He figured that since she lived in Watson, that she came from nothing, she'd be more than willing to put out for him. More than thrilled to have just a few minutes of his precious time.

Before she could verbalize her thoughts or ask him to drive her home, Travis motioned to someone unseen. They weren't alone? Suddenly, a giant light flashed on the building in front of them. The entire side of it became a massive movie screen.

He'd created his own drive-in, for two. Maya looked at him, overwhelmed.

"I wasn't sure what kind of movies you liked," he said. "So I went for a Peyton Smith movie. I don't know if it's any good—it hasn't come out yet. But girls like him, right?" Peyton Smith was like a young Ryan Gosling, all sophisticated smolder and Bambi eyes. Yes, girls liked him. But something told Maya even he'd be intimidated by Travis Reed right now.

Travis put his arm around her, drawing her close. He smelled amazing.

It was the perfect scene. The perfect night. So why hadn't Maya loosened up yet?

"Check out the glove compartment," Travis said.

Maya did. Movie snacks poured out.

"I was going to bring popcorn, but the popper wouldn't fit in my trunk," he said, smiling.

"Who needs popcorn?" Maya asked. "It's just corn. That's popped. With heat." Maya hated herself. She hated everything that was coming out of her mouth. "I'm sorry," she said, her whole face changing. "I can't do this."

"You can't do what?" Travis asked.

"This, this date," Maya said. "Whatever this is." Suddenly, everything that Maya had been bottling up unloaded like a shaken can of soda. And it exploded all over their night.

"I've never been on a date before," she confessed. "I mean, a couple times I went places or whatever, but hello, this? I don't know what to do. I'm so nervous I can't even speak actual sentences. 'Popcorn is just corn that's popped'—what is that? I'm actually kind of a smart person, but you'd never know it. I was babbling at the restaurant. I'm literally shaking here. Look."

She showed him her hand. It was shaking, all right.

"And it's not just the dating thing. You're Travis Reed. It's just a name to you, but to me it's a mythical creature I've built up in my head like Godzilla or Santa Claus, and now I'm having this crazy, romantic night with you, and I can't even enjoy it. Because it feels like I'm on some other girl's date. Who am I?" She couldn't stop right now if she tried. "Don't get me wrong, I have self-esteem, but, I mean . . . Travis Reed! Travis Reed, who is now looking at me like I just escaped from the insane asylum and I don't know why I vomited all this up all over you and I'm still talking and I can't for the life of me—"

Travis held her hands, stopping her. He wasn't running away like she'd assumed he would. Instead, he looked at her with an intense amount of . . . was that sympathy?

"Oh wow," she said. It was sympathy. "I'm so embarrassed."

"Don't be," he said finally. "You're not the one who had to be a show-off."

"A show-off?" Maya had no idea what he was talking about.

"Did you not see the restaurant I took you to?" Travis asked. "We were the youngest people there by, like, thirty years."

"I thought it was nice," she said.

"You were supposed to," he responded. "Just like you were supposed to be blown away by this drive-in and tell all your friends about all this amazing stuff I did for you. You care too much about what I think. I care too much about what everyone else thinks. So it looks like we're both messes."

It was the first real moment on their entire date. Actually, the entire time they'd known each other. This was Travis Reed the person, not Travis Reed the legend.

"Your hands aren't shaking anymore," he said, still holding on to them.

She smiled. "I guess you warmed them up."

For the next hour and a half, they watched the movie and laughed. They cracked jokes. And they gorged on the snacks he'd brought, which were way better than mussels.

Finally, the movie ended. As the sound of the spinning film reel echoed in the parking lot, there was nothing left to do but drive back to campus. But instead, they sat there. Maya knew what was coming next. Travis would make his grandest gesture yet. He would kiss her.

It would be a kiss, she resolved, that would wash that one with he who shall remain nameless out of her mind.

Bathed in the white light of the projector, she got her wish. Travis kissed her. Mission accomplished. And then some.

Chapter 10

"I'm sorry, a drive-in?" Cleo asked. "In the middle of a parking lot?"

Maya sat on the quad with Cleo and Renee recounting every last juicy detail of her date. She knew it sounded crazy. "I'm telling you, we pulled in and it was just the abandoned parking lot, and I swear to God I thought all he wanted to do was have sex with me."

"Which would've been bad why?" Renee asked. Cleo swatted her.

"We kissed after the movie, though," Maya said, ignoring Renee. "After he told me how obsessed he was with impressing me . . ."

Renee's jaw dropped.

"That never happened," Cleo said.

"Believe it or don't believe it, I don't care," Maya said. "As much as I sweated through that fancy dress, I still wouldn't change a thing about last night. It's the beginning of a beautiful love story, mark my words." Suddenly, Maya mocked hearing something in the distance. "Wait, do you hear that . . . ?"

Cleo and Renee got quiet.

"Wedding bells," Maya whispered.

They all laughed. Maya had never been at the center of even a halfway juicy story, so she couldn't help enjoying it. And wringing it out for every last ounce it was worth.

"Seriously," Renee said. "Why didn't you have sex with him?" Maya and Cleo just laughed some more.

"Have sex with who?" Travis appeared out of nowhere.

"Nobody," Maya jumped, red-faced. She tried to make a quick recovery. "Renee was asking, uh . . . Cleo, about . . . someone who's not here."

Recovery fail.

"Okay, then," Travis said. He obviously had more important business at hand. "You got a second?"

"Yeah," she replied. He pulled her away, but Maya could see a nosy Cleo and Renee eavesdropping on every word.

"Last night was . . ." He just smiled.

"Yeah," Maya agreed. His smile was infectious.

"I hope this doesn't sound weird but . . . it will," Travis said, poised with a question.

Cleo and Renee angled in more.

"Do you want to hang out again tonight?"

"Sure," she said. "What's so weird about that?"

"At my dad's," he added. "He wants to meet you."

"He wants to meet me?" Maya asked, dumbstruck. "He's

already met me. Twice. The last time, he kicked me out of the Academy, remember? You were there . . . ?"

"That was Maya the troublemaking rebel," he said. "This is Maya the girl I went out on a date with."

Cleo and Renee scooched over so close they were nearly sitting on Maya's and Travis's laps. Maya shot them a look.

"I don't mean to be Maya the moron but . . . isn't meeting the parents after one date kind of . . . ?" She searched for the right word.

"Insane? That's just my dad," Travis said. "You can say no."

"No," Maya said. "I mean, no to saying no. I'd love to hang out again."

Travis beamed. "Cool. I'll text you where and when. See you tonight." He took off.

Maya stood there smiling. Until he was a safe distance away, anyway. Then she turned back to Cleo and Renee with her eyes bugging out of her head.

"You would not believe what he just asked me—" Maya started to say.

"Yeah, yeah, we heard the whole thing," Renee said.

Cleo shook her head. "I'm sorry I ever doubted you. Meeting the parents!"

"Parent," Maya corrected, in a daze. "Mom's traveling around Europe."

"She's already calling her Mom," Renee said.

"That's not what I meant," Maya said. "This is weird. This is weird, right? This is weird." Maya thought of her meetings with Nails in the past.

"Relax," Cleo said. "It's just dinner. So what if blowing it with Nails means you'll never go on another date with his son ever again?"

"Stop that!" Maya said.

"I'm sorry, bad joke," Cleo said, smiling.

It was a bad joke. But for the rest of the afternoon, it haunted Maya. Because there was truth in it. As far as Travis was concerned, the sun rose and set on his father. If she didn't pass Nails's test, it would definitely affect the way Travis felt about her. It had to. Maya couldn't help but think that this was over before it began.

As she got ready for dinner (7 p.m. sharp!), Maya prepared herself. She looked amazing, she'd rehearsed several speeches about how important respecting the rules of the Academy was, and she'd Listerined. She would be ready for anything tonight.

Except, that is, the location of the dinner.

The off-campus address Travis had texted her was no restaurant. It was Nails Reed's home. Correction, Nails Reed's megamansion.

It took Maya a solid five minutes to make her way from the gate to the front door. And though she'd already announced her presence to security so they'd open the gate, she still contemplated running away the minute she rang the bell.

Before she could act on that all-so-familiar impulse to run, the door opened and she was greeted by a sturdy housekeeper.

"Come in," the woman said, ushering her inside. "They're waiting for you in the study."

Was she late? She tried to find a clock, to no avail. Apparently rich people didn't need to know the time.

The housekeeper escorted her through the house en route to the study. Maya felt like she was in line for an amusement-park ride and wondered if there was a Fastpass. Or at least a handy foldout map.

They arrived in the study, where Travis and Nails stood hunched over a desk.

"Hi," Maya said as she stood at the entryway, needing to clear her throat before she was able to get the whole word out.

"Hey," Travis said, lighting up. "Dad, you remember Maya."

"Of course," Nails said. "The sliding and entering girl."

Oh God, Maya thought. Really? The second she got there?

Nails studied her. "You look a little different since you were in my office."

"Actually, you never brought me in," Maya said. "You sat me outside."

"Well, I was afraid you'd steal something else of mine," he said.

Everything Maya dreaded would happen throughout the course of the evening was apparently all happening within the first thirty seconds of her arrival.

"I'm kidding," Nails said. "Come in, make yourself comfortable."

As if that were even possible.

"My dad was just teaching me some plays," Travis said. He stepped back from the desk, revealing dozens of Post-its marked with Xs and Os.

"Do you know anything about football, Maya?" Nails asked.

Crap! Maya prepared for every question under the sun but that one. The only Xs and Os Maya used were in texts with Cleo, and even those were sarcastic.

"Oh, well," she said, "my dad's a big fan." It wasn't an answer, but she'd hoped it would be enough for Nails.

"Who's your favorite player?" Nails asked.

"You?" Everyone was silent. Until Nails laughed.

"She's got good taste," Nails told his son. Maya exhaled. And then she beamed when she saw Travis look at her with even more appreciative eyes. All this time she had been trying to impress Travis. Clearly it was Nails she should've been trying to win over.

"I hope you brought your appetite," Nails said. "Pretty sure Butler slaughtered a pig for us." Butler was the chef, which made no sense to Maya. But like her father always said, poor people were crazy, but rich people were eccentric. So it was okay.

Nails led them to the dining room. Between the crystal, the flowers, and the silverware, it looked like the table was made up for royalty. How was eating here even comfortable?

Travis helped Maya to her seat as the first course was brought out like clockwork. The dish was some weird scallop thing Maya again couldn't pronounce. One for her, one for Travis, and one for Nails. Two more were placed on the table.

"Are we waiting for someone?" Maya asked.

"Always," Travis replied.

Just then, he made his way in. It was Jake, with a stripper.

Of course, his date was too young to be a stripper, but it was clearly her ambition to look like one. Teased hair, short skirt, more makeup than a rodeo clown.

Maya braced herself.

"Did I miss the snooty appetizer?" Jake asked. His date laughed. At least Maya thought it was a laugh. It could've been one of those high-pitched sneezes that went on for too long. "This is Mandy."

"Mindy," she corrected. But she didn't seem to mind.

Jake spotted Maya. "I remember you."

Maya forced a smile but said nothing. The less interaction she had with him, the better.

Jake and his date sat. Maya was bugged that he was crashing their evening, but having Mindy there was another story. There was no way Maya could do anything but dazzle with this chick sitting at the table with them.

"Why weren't you at practice this morning?" Travis asked.

Nails looked at Jake sharply. "You skipped practice?"

"Food poisoning," Jake said.

"Or alcohol, right?" Mindy laughed again (yeah, definitely a laugh).

"Mandy's joking," Jake said.

"Mindy," she corrected. She still didn't mind.

Mindy/Mandy had gone from useful to downright entertaining.

"How did you two meet?" Maya asked Jake, trying to keep a straight face. The entertainment value in needling Jake outweighed her desire to stay quiet. It also had the added benefit of showing Nails whose side she was on.

"We'd much rather hear how your date went last night," Jake replied. "I hear Travis took you to a parking lot."

"A drive-in movie, actually," Maya shot back, trying to maintain her ladylike demeanor in front of her host. "You know, those things that don't exist anymore. Travis made it exist."

"He's good at making something out of nothing." Jake smiled.

Maya wondered how much damage her fork would do if she jammed it into Jake's hand.

"It's called effort," Nails said to Jake pointedly. "You'd be amazed what a little of that can get you." He turned to Maya. "One of my sons inherited my work ethic. The other . . . I don't know what he inherited of mine, frankly." He looked to Travis, his facial expression becoming much kinder. "What movie did you watch?"

"It was a dance movie," Travis said. "It comes out next month."

"Are you a fan of dance?" Nails asked Maya.

"Yeah," Maya said. "But I couldn't do any of those moves to save my life. It was all this salsa and samba, and . . . bolero . . . ?" Maya asked Travis.

"Bolero," Travis confirmed.

"It was like their hips were on hinges or something," Maya continued. "I've always wanted to be that girl, you know? She walks in and just—bam—with the hips." Maya did a little wiggle in her seat. And then she felt everyone's eyes on her. Including Jake, who had a dumb grin on his face.

"But, you know . . . ," Maya said sheepishly. "That's not

me." She prayed for Mindy to do something horrifying to steal the spotlight.

"Dinner was great, Mr. Nails," Mindy said. "I'm stuffed."

Oh, thank you, Maya thought. She really should have Mindy on payroll.

Nails just looked at Jake. He didn't have to say anything to show what a complete and total idiot he thought this girl was. To make the point further, he shifted his entire focus to Maya.

"What do your parents do for a living, Maya?" Nails asked.

"Oh," Maya blurted. "Um, my dad's a . . . small-business owner." The last thing Maya wanted to talk about while sitting in this million-dollar banquet room was her used-pickup-truck-driving family.

"What kind of business?" Jake asked.

Maya shot him a look. "Landscape architecture." It sounded a lot better than saying he mowed people's lawns for cash.

"What about your mom?" Jake asked. He wouldn't leave her alone.

"She's a domestic engineer," Maya said.

"A housewife," Jake clarified.

"Our mom's a housewife," Travis said to Jake.

"Our mom's a professional tourist," Jake shot back.

Their mother wasn't just a sore spot for Travis, she was a sore spot for both of them. But Maya couldn't figure out exactly what was being said there. She did know that when Butler the chef brought the main course, his timing couldn't have been any better. The tension was so thick it could've been cut with the giant steak knives that were placed by their sides.

"Pork chops," Jake said. "My favorite."

"I thought they were Travis's favorite?" Nails said. They were, Jake was making a point. So was Nails. What cracked-out family drama had Maya walked into?

Dinner continued this way, with Jake acting bratty and Nails putting him in his place. That place was usually located somewhere beneath Travis. Travis's focus, meanwhile, was on Maya and making sure she was comfortably out of the fray.

Dessert was amazing. Maya didn't know what it was called, but it was pear and it was on fire, so it worked for her. It obviously worked for Jake and Travis, who began to wolf down theirs at an alarming speed. The flames hadn't even gone out yet.

"What are you doing?" Maya asked them both.

"Ignore it," Nails said. "They've done this all the time since they were little kids. Whoever finished their meals first won."

"Won what?" Maya asked, but before Nails could answer, Travis slammed his fist on the table.

"Done!" Travis announced proudly.

Jake tossed his spoon down in disgust.

"Bragging rights," Nails finally answered.

"If we weren't on the same team," Travis said, "I'm pretty sure he'd tackle me to my death."

"I'd let you live," Jake said, smiling. "How else would you know I wrecked you?"

"The only sport I know how to play is rock, paper, scissors," Mindy said. "I lose a lot."

"That's not really a sport, Mandy," Jake said. Mindy didn't even bother to correct him this time.

"It could be," Travis said. It was a challenge. One Jake arched his eyebrow over. And then gladly accepted.

"You're on," Jake said.

They threw out their hands and started.

"One, two, three, go!" Jake said. Travis won. "One, two, three, go!" Jake said again. Again Travis won.

"Okay, that was fun—" Maya started to say, but Travis and Jake just continued. "Guys, you can't be taking this this seriously. . . ." But they were. She looked to Nails to share an eyeroll at their expense, but he was totally into it, too. Especially every time Travis won. It was unsettling.

"One, two, three, go! One, two, three, go!" Jake got louder and louder, his eyes wilder and wilder. Travis was as steady and calm as they came. He was reading everything Jake was doing before he was doing it.

"See Travis thinking there?" Nails asked Maya. "That's a champion's mentality there. That one's going places."

"This is rigged!" Jake said. "Okay, last one takes all."

"Care to make it interesting?" Travis asked.

Maya didn't think that was possible.

"What did you have in mind?" Jake asked.

"I win, you can't miss practice for a month," Travis said.

"And if I win?"

"You can have this whole house to yourself one night to throw a huge party." It was Nails this time. He was not only rooting for Travis, he was for all intents and purposes betting against Jake.

"Deal," Jake said.

"One, two, three, go!" Nails said, firmly a part of the action. Jake threw down rock. Travis threw down paper.

Jake let out a monster yell. A great big, make-everyone-uncomfortable roar.

"That's the difference," Nails said, charged. "Travis is steady. Jake is ruled by his emotions. One gets you the win, the other makes you lose."

Jake just pounded the table, then stormed out.

"See you at practice!" Travis called after him.

"Thank you for a lovely evening," Jake's date said as she got up, adjusted her skirt, then ran after him.

Nails chuckled. "I guess that's the end of dinner." He got up and made his way over to Maya. "Maya, it's been great to spend some time with you. I can see why Travis wanted me to invite you over so badly."

"Travis wanted . . . ?" Maya looked at Travis, confused.

"Thanks for not stealing anything," Nails added before bidding them good night and leaving them alone.

"I thought your dad was the one who insisted I come over?" Maya asked.

Travis smiled sheepishly. Busted. Maya didn't think he should feel weird about it. On the contrary, it made her swoon.

"What are you doing tomorrow?" Travis said, eager to move on from the subject.

"I'm not sure. Probably practice. The usual," Maya replied.

"I'd love it if you'd take a quick trip off campus with me," he said. "If tonight didn't scare you off."

Maya didn't hesitate. "I'd love to."

"Great," Travis said.

Travis drove Maya back to campus and dropped her off. But not before kissing her again.

As Maya climbed the humble steps of Watson back to her room, she didn't know how she'd done it. Not only had she survived dinner, she'd scored her third date with Travis Reed in three days.

If dating were a sport, she'd be a world champion.

Chapter 11

Maya didn't know what kind of quick trip Travis had in mind, but somehow it involved picking her up in front of Watson at six in the morning. He'd offered to come upstairs and retrieve her like a gentleman, but she was afraid Cleo would've swung a nine iron into his face for waking her up when it was still pitch-black out.

"Where are we going?" Maya asked as she got in his car. She wiped the sleep from her eyes, though it was really for dramatic effect, as she'd been up for an hour making herself look flawless.

"It's a surprise," Travis said.

"I just have to warn you, I have a really bad track record with surprises," Maya informed him. "There have been injuries."

"What kind of injuries?" Travis asked as he turned onto the highway ramp.

"Let's just say there's a reason my father never had any more children after me," Maya said pointedly.

He laughed. "I'll take my chances."

Travis took an exit, the sign for which Maya was convinced she'd read wrong.

"The airport?" Maya asked. "What's at the airport?"

Travis grinned. "Airplanes, of course."

Travis parked, and in a whirlwind Maya found herself standing outside something that never even crossed her mind: the Academy's private plane.

"Okay, you think I'm joking," Maya said. "But I'm not going to be able to stop myself from crippling you if you don't tell me what's going on this instant."

"Mr. Reed," the pilot said as he opened the door of the plane. He lowered the steps.

"Travis," Maya said, "I'm not getting on that plane unless you tell me what's going on."

"You have serious trust issues," he said.

Maya had serious moving issues. As in, she wasn't moving off that spot unless Travis told her what was happening.

Finally, having no other choice, he told her. "I'm taking you for a lesson."

Maya scrunched her face. Lessons. She hadn't expressed any interest in flying. This was just some other random rich-people activity she didn't get at all, like eating cucumber sandwiches or going to horse races just to wear the stupid hats. But it could be cool. So she relented.

As they ascended, Maya waited for the pilot to call her up to the cockpit. Five thousand feet. Ten thousand feet. Fifteen thousand feet. Patience wasn't Maya's strong suit, either, so when they hit twenty thousand feet, she turned to Travis, who flipped lazily through a magazine.

"When am I grabbing the wheel?" she asked him.

"What are you talking about?" He flipped a page.

"The wheel, the stick, whatever you steer this thing with," she said. "When does my lesson start?"

Travis laughed. "Maya, I'm not giving flying lessons. I'm not suicidal."

Now she was really confused. "What are we doing, then?"

"I told you," he said. "We're taking a quick trip."

Maya's eyes went wide. "You're taking me somewhere? Like, away? Where?!"

"If I told you, it wouldn't be a surprise," he said.

"And if you don't tell me, it's kidnapping," she said. "How can you fly us anywhere? We didn't go through airport security. I didn't show a single person my ID."

"Remember that guy with the clipboard?" he asked.

Maya vaguely remembered Travis sharing all of five words with a guy when they came in. "That was it?"

"Different rules for different people, Maya." It was the exact same thing Cleo had said when Maya got kicked out for the Great Framed-Poster Heist and Nicole walked away scot-free. Maya was the "different people" now, and she kind of liked it.

But she was still on a plane going who knows where.

"Do you trust me?" Travis asked.

She thought about it. "You won't even give me a hint of where we're going?"

He mimed sealing his lips.

She considered. "You're lucky I don't know how to work a parachute."

Travis smiled. They continued on to destinations unknown, Maya wondering what she'd gotten herself into until the early-morning hour caught up to her and she fell back asleep.

"Maya, Maya, we're here." Travis was leaning over her.

Maya woke up slowly. "How long was I out for?" She suddenly became acutely aware of her breath and did everything to avoid talking in his direction until she could locate a piece of gum.

"Not long," he said.

The pilot opened the door and ushered them onto the tarmac, where a limo waited. Maya had never stepped foot in a limo. The driver greeted them cheerfully. *"Bem-vindo,"* he said.

Maya looked at Travis, alarmed. *"Bem-vindo? Bem-vindo's* not English."

"No, it is not," he said, a devilish look in his eyes.

"You took me out of the country?!" Maya blurted. "How did you do that without my passport?"

Travis held a copy of her passport up.

"The Academy keeps everyone's on file," he said. "You know, because of all the traveling we do to international competitions." All she could do was shake her head.

"Shall we?" Travis helped her into the limo, and they drove off. Maya should've been studying everything inside, but her eyes were darting everywhere outside looking for the smallest clue to where they could be.

The farther they got from the airport, the more beautiful the view. By the time she saw beaches, she knew. The Bahamas was a quick plane ride away—kids talked about taking flights over all the time. It was obviously her turn, and she couldn't be happier.

"You know where we are, don't you?" Travis asked.

She didn't know what to say. "Travis, you're too much."

And then she saw it. It was a road sign with three little words that blew her mind to pieces.

Rio de Janeiro.

"Rio de . . . ?" When she could think again, Maya whipped her face to Travis's. "Rio de Janeiro? *We're in Rio de Janeiro?*"

Travis beamed.

"This is a little trip? You took me to Brazil!" Though the roof of the limo was a mere foot from the top of her head she managed to stand. "Travis, I have school. I know you can do whatever you want, but I can't. I'm on scholarship; scholarship kids can't fly down to Brazil—"

"Maya, you're with the son of the Academy owner," he said. "I don't want to sound like a schmuck here, but, you know . . . you'll be fine." She wasn't totally convinced. "I have this all planned out. We're overnighting it back. You'll barely miss a thing, I promise. Enjoy yourself. You're in Rio!"

She was. She was in Rio. And it made absolutely no sense to her whatsoever. In this moment, she might as well have been on the moon.

"Admit this is cool," he said. "Admit it or I'll take you right back to the airport this minute and we'll fly home now." It was like he needed her to be blown away. When she couldn't leap on it, he rolled down the windows and motioned to the gorgeous beaches as they drove past. Music filled the air as people went about their daily business flashing unbelievable amounts of skin. There was a guy jogging in a Speedo, a woman pumping gas in a bikini and flip-flops.

Travis motioned toward the mountains above them, where a giant Christ statue held its arms open wide, embracing the entire city.

"Okay," Maya said begrudgingly. "It's cool."

"It's like pulling teeth!" Travis said.

Finally, Maya broke. "Yes! Okay, of course it's cool—are you kidding me?" Maya said. "This is amazing, it's just . . . Travis, it's too much. Too much for me. I don't . . ."

"Deserve it?" Travis asked.

"I'm not saying that," Maya said. But she was kind of saying it. "It's just more than . . ." She didn't know how to say it. "Travis, I'm not used to this."

"Don't worry," he said, calming her. "We're just going to see one little part of Rio. Nothing too crazy."

"What part?" she asked.

"This part," he said. The limo pulled over in front of a storefront dance studio. A woman with a deep tan and a long dress was waiting for them.

"What is this?" Maya asked.

"I told you I was taking you for a lesson," he said. When she didn't say anything, he continued. "You said it was your dream to learn how to samba, to walk into a room and be, like, 'bam' with your hips. . . ." He did the little move she did at dinner. "Flavia de Souza is the best samba teacher in the world. She's going to teach us."

Maya stood there. "You brought me to Rio to give me a dance lesson?"

"No," he said. "To give *us* a dance lesson."

Rio suddenly paled in comparison to this moment right here.

"Shall we?" Travis asked, reaching for her hand. She smiled as he led her to Flavia, and their lesson.

Flavia was the most emotional woman Maya had ever met. Every breath she took was dramatic. Every step filled with passion. But it was all completely elegant. Maya was not born with elegance, so Flavia made it her mission to draw it out of her.

At first, Flavia danced with Maya alone, leading her through the steps of a samba. Somehow, dancing with this strange woman seemed like the most natural thing on earth. Maya went from plodding along the floor to gliding with the music.

"Look at you!" Travis beamed. He was going through the steps with Flavia's assistant, and doing okay. He was perfect at a lot of things, but dancing was something that seemed to require his total concentration.

"You are doing the steps," Flavia told Travis. "But you are not feeling them. Come." She stepped aside and handed Maya to him like an offering.

Travis and Maya clasped hands.

"She's not a rake. You are not doing, how do you say, the

yard work," Flavia said, moving them closer. "Hold her like this."

Travis and Maya started to dance. With the wild music and the wilder hip swings, Maya felt so out of her element. By the look on his face, she suspected Travis did, too. But they were out of their element together.

"Feel the steps," Flavia said, dancing with them from behind Maya. "Don't worry about being perfect. Perfect is boring. Perfect is death!"

They continued to dance.

"I'm sorry," Travis said. "My hips aren't on hinges." He was genuinely apologetic.

"We can be awful together," Maya said. She liked that Travis had a flaw. And that, while he might not have been the best, he seemed to be doing his best to enjoy it. It made her enjoy it.

"Now what?" Maya asked.

"Now," he said, "I have a little business to do down here." He took off his shirt and dried himself with a towel.

"Business?" Maya asked, looking away as if he were flashing her. She still sneaked a glance or five in the mirrors that lined the walls.

"My dad has a hot prospect down here," Travis said. "A sixteen-year-old soccer player from the slums." *The slums*? Maya thought. *Are they allowed to say that?* "I'm supposed to meet up with him tonight, schmooze him a little."

"Who'd need schmoozing to come to the Academy?" Maya asked.

"His name is Diego," he said. "His family is poor, so some

lesser academies are throwing a ton of cash at him. But they're not going to do for him what we can do for him. I need to let him know that. Over dinner, so I hope you're hungry."

"Wait a minute," Maya said, taking a second for the truth to sink in. "This trip wasn't about me; this trip was about him."

"Couldn't it be both?" Travis asked.

Travis really was wily. But Maya could only be impressed. And, frankly, a little relieved this wasn't all about her. But he wanted her there, which was really all she needed to know.

"I don't have anything to wear for dinner," Maya said. "This was all I brought, and it's drenched."

"Leave that to me," he said, smiling.

They said good-bye to Flavia and left the studio, but instead of getting back into the limo, Travis walked her a few blocks down the road, to a high-end boutique on the corner.

"Have you ever seen *Pretty Woman*?" Travis opened the door, then ushered her inside, where the owner waited.

"She's even taller than you said she'd be," the woman marveled.

At first confused, Maya realized what he was planning. "You're not taking me on a shopping spree."

"Of course not," Travis said. "The Academy is." He whipped out a credit card. "It is a business trip, after all."

The woman and her assistants swooped in and took all of Maya's measurements.

"Travis, no," Maya said.

"In order to get your scholarship, you agreed to give the Academy a cut of all your potential future earnings," he said, sounding ever the businessman. "So in actuality, you're really the one paying for this."

Wily, wily, wily.

"It's too much," she said. "Travis, at some point you're going to have to stop."

"You're right," he said. "Just not today." He handed the saleswoman the credit card. "Now, you've seen the movie—you have to go model the clothes, and I do the whole thumbs-up, thumbs-down thing."

"You're insane," she said.

"Less talkin', more thumbin'."

Maya laughed. "Do you always win?"

"Always," he said.

With that, Maya was led to the dressing room to try on the first of many outfits. She would walk out the door with most of them.

Travis and Maya sat with Diego at a private booth in the most expensive restaurant in Rio. Maya could see why the Academy was so interested in this kid. Besides the fact that he was legitimately a phenom on the soccer field, he was a phenom in the looks department as well. He had eyelashes for days, curly dark hair a girl could lose her fingers in, and teeth handcrafted by God to sell toothpaste. He also had an innate ability to make everyone he interacted with feel like they were the only person on earth. He was a star, and he was going to make someone a lot of money.

"Another drink for my friend here," Travis said to the

waiter before turning his attention back to Diego. "Diego, listen. I get it. You have needs. Your family has needs. And these other academies aren't just throwing promises at you, they're also throwing cash. But those promises are empty, and that cash will eventually run out. Then where will your family be?"

Diego was listening, Maya could tell. But beyond that, she couldn't read him.

"You're worried about them," Travis continued. "But you also have to worry about you. These other places can't give you what we can. Top-notch facilities, world-class coaches. At the Academy, you won't just have a field to run around on, you'll actually get better. You could become the best."

Maya was impressed. If she played soccer, she'd sign up on the spot. Diego just leaned back.

"I've seen a lot of people from a lot of academies," Diego said finally. "But you're the only one I've seen who's my age." He said it almost conspiratorially. "Your father sent you for a reason."

He was right. Until now, Maya hadn't even questioned why Nails would send a seventeen-year-old—even one as capable as Travis—to do a job so huge. Not only that but also send him alone. Travis was a tool to gain Diego's trust. Maya realized right then and there how smart Nails was. When Travis didn't flinch at Diego's observation, it was clear he was in on the plan. Which only made him that much more impressive. She felt like she was sitting at the big boys' table.

"My father wanted you to see a success story," Travis said. "When I enter the NFL draft, I'll have a number one next to my name, and you can be sure it's because I went to the Academy."

Diego studied him. "I know the Academy is where I need to be," he said. "You don't need to convince me of that."

Travis smiled. "So . . . welcome to the Academy?"

Diego hesitated. There was something holding him back.

"What?" Travis said. "We love you, you love us. What's the problem? Is it girls you want? We've got plenty of those."

Maya studied Diego. She recognized that look in his eyes. He was as uncomfortable in this extravagant restaurant as Maya was on her first date with Travis. The overwhelmed look behind his eyes matched every overwhelmed look Maya had had with Travis since, from their first date to the trip to Rio. Travis meant well, but his need to impress didn't factor in the emotions of others. It could wind up being a much bigger flaw for him than anything his hips weren't able to do.

"Diego," Maya said, leaning in, "I get it. This dog and pony show, it's a little ridiculous."

"Maya . . . ," Travis warned.

"Can't you see you're freaking him out?" Maya asked. "Diego, you're worried that he doesn't understand you. Well, you're right, he doesn't."

"Diego, will you excuse us?" Travis started to stand, but Maya just put her hand on his, calming him down for a change.

"He doesn't understand you," Maya said, staying on Diego. "But plenty of other kids at the Academy do. My best friend's entire family is hanging everything on her, on her going pro, making all this money and rescuing them from the shack they live in. The pressure is insane. And she's not the only one there who feels it. But you'll feel it anywhere. At least at the Academy, you'll have people who can get you there. If you're willing to work for it."

Diego just looked at her. Then he stood up, loosened his tie, and undid his top button, which was so tight around his neck it left a mark.

"Yeah, sorry, I need to get out of here," Diego said. He turned to go, then turned back to Travis. "You can tell your father you did a good job."

Travis perked up. "A good job or a great job?"

Diego just shook his head. "You'll do a great job when you get me signed by a killer team for a lot of zeroes. I need a month or so to tie things up here. See you soon." Diego smiled, then walked out.

Maya smiled bigger. "You did it!"

"We did it," Travis said, even more elated. "Maya, you don't even know how much that kid is worth. You were amazing."

"*You* were amazing," she said.

He just studied her. "I knew you were beautiful, I knew you were nice, but . . . we actually make a great team."

As much as Diego's words meant to Travis, Travis's words meant that much and more to Maya. A team, he'd said. It sent a surge up her spine.

"We should probably get going, too," he said. "Little bit of a ride back."

She didn't want this day to end. But it had to eventually.

"Maybe we could samba on the plane?" he asked.

Maya smiled. "I'd like that."

They flew back to the Academy, sleeping away the overnight flight. Maya didn't dream. She didn't have to.

Chapter 12

Maya sat in class while her teacher Mr. Manjarrez droned on. He was a humorless man with a face that looked like he'd just sucked on an under-ripe grapefruit. As he filled the room with white noise, Maya caught a pair of eyes dart back in her direction. She felt another from the far side of the room. What was going on beside her that was so interesting? She looked over and made a shocking realization: *All these eyes were stealing glimpses of her.* It was the absolute strangest sensation, one she didn't know what to do with at all.

"Have you heard from him?" Cleo asked, leaning forward from the desk behind her.

Maya tried to shake off all the attention. "He sent me this," she whispered, then sneaked her phone behind her back to reveal a text from Travis. It was a smiley face.

"Watch your back, Shakespeare," Cleo cracked. Maya snatched it back. Cleo didn't deserve to see his text.

"Ladies," Mr. Manjarrez said, "if you can tell me how many pages this paper has to be, I'll give you an A on it right here and now."

"Paper?" Maya asked.

"Ten pages!" Cleo guessed desperately.

"Twelve," he said, self-satisfied. "On the Bay of Pigs. Which I just explained was an invasion of . . . ? Another chance, B-plus . . . ?" They stared at him blankly. "Wonderful. Good luck to you both."

Just then, the intercom chimed. "Maya Hart to Mr. Reed's office, please."

Maya looked to Cleo, panicked.

"What did you do?" Cleo asked, hushed.

Maya had no idea. But the woman's voice was not friendly. Maya gathered her things slowly, delaying the inevitable. Finally, after a look of encouragement from Cleo that even Cleo didn't seem to believe, Maya went on her way.

Maya was seated in Nails's office. She didn't know if this was better or worse than her last visit, when she never made it past the doorway. The office was a museum to all his accomplishments on the field, the prized items being the three Super Bowl rings encased on the wall, each hanging over an MVP trophy. Gracing the other walls were photos of Nails with celebrities and politicians, including four with US presidents and one with the Dalai Lama. They were all gawking at Nails, not the other way around. But he would be intimidating even with the walls bare. That power was something he carried with him wherever he went. And right now, facing him, she was scared witless. She'd had a lovely dinner with him in his home mere days ago, and by the look on his face, you'd never know it.

"Maya, I can't be delicate about this," Nails said finally. "You're here because of a photograph. A revealing photograph that was posted online."

Maya went ashen. She thought that photo of Nicole had been forgotten. Obviously Nicole had told him about it. She'd told him Maya took that picture of her in the shower, that it was her who'd posted it. Last time was a warning; this time she was done.

"I didn't know that was going to happen," Maya said. "I swear. I would've done anything to take it offline, but it's the Internet. Once it's up there . . ."

"That's all well and good," Nails said. "But what's done is done. There are rules here, and those rules were broken."

"So . . . that's it?" Maya asked. "You're kicking me out?"

Nails was confused. "Why would I kick you out for something she did?" he asked.

"Something she . . . ?" Now Maya was confused.

Oh God, Maya thought. He was kicking Cleo out. She couldn't let him do it. She wouldn't. If that meant sacrificing herself, that's what she would do.

"I can't let you do that," she said.

"You don't have a choice," he said. "It was Christine who'd put this picture of herself online," he said, turning his laptop so she could see. "She's got to face the consequences." Maya recognized the girl on the screen. She'd seen photos of her in the girl's bedroom. It was Nicole and Renee's forever-absent third roommate. And when it came to the photo, *revealing* was a gross understatement. "I hope it was worth the attention she got, because she's gone."

It took a minute for Maya's heart to slow down. Cleo wasn't in trouble. Neither was she. But then, she thought, why was she here? In his office? And in the middle of class, no less?

"What this means," Nails said, "is that there's a vacancy in the villa. It's a vacancy I thought you could fill."

She couldn't have heard that right. "Me? I can't afford the villa. I can't even afford the parking space for the villa." This wasn't news. So why was Nails even suggesting it?

"Consider it our investment in you," he said. "I've also removed your six-month probationary period. You're here to stay."

She was having a stroke. That would explain it.

"What," he said. "No response?" For the first time, he looked like the guy she'd had dinner with.

"No, I'm . . . I don't know how to describe it," she stammered. "Staying is all I want, but . . . Why are you doing this? Is it because of Travis? Because I've been hanging out with him?"

"I don't do anything for personal reasons, Maya. And neither should you." With that, he took out a box cutter and opened a cardboard box on his desk. Inside were hundreds of freshly printed books with the Academy logo on them. He took one out and slid it to her. It was the new welcome packet.

On the cover was a gorgeous girl Maya didn't recognize. Until she looked closer.

"Is that . . . me?" Maya asked. It was from the impromptu photo shoot she had done with that Academy photographer outside the courts. She didn't know what that guy did to create the girl she was looking at, but she was stunning.

"It is," he said. "Results are important to a career, Maya, but image can be just as powerful. This girl here is beautiful to guys without being threatening to girls. She's sweet but strong. She's aspirational. Aspirational sells. I'm offering you a spot in the villa partly to say thanks."

" 'Partly'?" Maya asked, still processing it all.

"Mostly," he said. "Because I like what I've been seeing of you lately."

Since she didn't remember seeing him at any of her practices, she wondered whom he was liking: the girl on the court or the girl off of it? She didn't ask, mostly because, deep down, she was afraid of what the answer might be.

"Thank you," she said.

With that, Maya left before he could change his mind.

Maya made her way back to Watson in a daze. As she walked up the stairs and unlocked her door, she barely noticed the blond who was on her way out. They exchanged polite smiles before Maya was inside, falling face-first onto Cleo's bed.

"Who was that?" Maya said, suddenly catching up with time.

"Who?" Cleo asked, engrossed in her laptop.

"That girl?" Maya said. "The one who just walked out of this room?"

Cleo hesitated, then answered. "Svetlana."

Maya sat up. "Like, Svetlana Svetlana? Svetlana-the-girl-you-kissed Svetlana?"

"Svetlana," Cleo said. "What happened when you were called down to the office?"

"Cleo!" Maya was on her feet, giddy. Way giddier than Cleo was. "She's so pretty."

"Is she?" Cleo asked. "We were just studying together."

Maya quickly looked over Cleo's shoulder. The laptop Cleo was so engrossed in wasn't even turned on. "Cleo."

"Okay, I heard you fumbling with your keys and I rushed her out. I'm just hanging out with her, like you said to. Seeing how I feel."

Maya sat back down. "So? How do you feel? Is Svetlana a good friend or, like, a *good* friend?"

"Well," Cleo said, "she's cute. Kind of funny. I just don't know."

"Did you kiss her again?" Maya asked. She couldn't be more in Cleo's business if she tried, and she didn't care.

"I was too chicken," Cleo said. "Which pisses me off because the one thing I'm not is chicken. The closer I get to this, the less I recognize myself."

Maya smiled. "Maybe you're just seeing yourself from a different angle."

Cleo took a second before continuing. "I invited Svetlana to movie night tomorrow. I know that's our thing, but

I was hoping you could be there to, I don't know, check her out. Plus, well, I don't think I'm ready for a one-on-one date."

"Of course she can come," Maya said.

The idea of movie night in their room the next day reminded Maya that she had to tell Cleo about the villa. And she had to tell her now.

"So, the office," Maya said. "Nails took my probationary period away."

"What? Why?" Cleo asked. "Is it because you've made out with both his kids?"

"No." Maya glared at her. "He said he liked what he's been seeing from me."

"Okay . . . ," Cleo responded.

There was no good way to say it. So she just did. "He also offered to move me into the villa. For free."

"Wow." Cleo didn't say anything else.

"I'm torn, like, really torn." Maya kneaded Cleo's blanket like dough. "I love our place. I love living with you." She meant every word.

"Maya," Cleo said, taking the blanket from her, "I would totally understand if you decided to do it. You'd be stupid not to. It's a palace. And to live there for free?"

"If I did it," Maya said, "you'd be over there so much, you'll think you live there, too."

"Well, hello?" Cleo said with a smile. "Can you imagine how much better movie night is going to be tomorrow on a one-hundred-and-fifty-two-inch flat screen?"

With Cleo urging her on, the decision was a no-brainer. Maya was moving into the villa.

Maya traded in her old metal key for a brand-new, fancy key card. She went straight to the villa, where, after a few unanswered knocks, she carefully swiped it in the electronic lock. With a click, the front door opened. It wasn't a dream after all. She carried her stuff inside.

She wasn't just visiting Wonka's factory, she was now living in it. It was a reality she couldn't grab on to.

The place was silent. Still. Even though it was her new home, she was afraid to make a sound. She found an iPad on the counter. Nicole and Renee used it just to leave messages for each other, their thousand-dollar dry-erase board. Typed on it in giant letters: "Welcome, Superstar! xx–Renee." Next to it was the welcome packet, with cover girl Maya circled with a red lipstick heart. Towering over it all was a giant bouquet of flowers with a card attached. They were from Travis. Maya lit up.

"I thought I heard someone," a voice said behind her.

Maya turned to find Nicole. She was in a towel, fresh from a shower.

Maya just stood there, unsure of how Nicole was going to react to having her there, in her home. Living with her. Time was at a crawl. Finally, Nicole smiled.

"Welcome, roomie." From Nicole, it was like a bear hug. And as big a greeting as Maya could've ever hoped for.

"Thanks," Maya said. "It's great to be here." It was perhaps the understatement of the century.

"It's a whole new world," Nicole said. "The only rule is there are no rules."

"Really?" Maya asked.

"No, not really," Nicole said. "There are tons of rules. I'll tell you them later." She smiled again, then headed back to her room to finish getting dressed.

It was a whole new world. A great big, beautiful new world. And Maya was ready.

Chapter 13

Maya was in the middle of the most amazing dream. She was dating a crown prince and living in a palace with the queen. She never wanted it to end. And it didn't, really. This was her life now.

Well, almost. Her bedroom still belonged to the girl who had it last. At least everything inside it did. She'd left all her furniture, her bedding—she'd even left her TV. In fact, it seemed like there was even more stuff in this room than when Maya was in it last.

Memories of the last time she was there infiltrated her brain. The darkness. The moonlight. Jake Reed's lips on hers. It had been right there in that corner. She would be sleeping in this same room every day. Reminded of it. Haunted by it.

Just then, there was a knock at her door.

"Rise and shine," Travis said, poking his head in. He had a

huge grin on his face. Maya smiled, too, both happy to see him and grateful to be wrenched from her memory.

"What are you doing here?" Maya asked, sitting up. Then she saw it, in his hands. A tray with a full-on breakfast spread, topped by a single daisy.

"We've got to start your time here off right," he said.

Maya just shook her head. "Does the villa come with its own Reed?"

"Just this room," he said. "Lucky you. Now, where's my tip?"

She kissed him.

"Don't make me get the fire hose." Renee walked in. She was still in her bathrobe, which was as red as Maya's face. "Well, hello, Travis. Fancy seeing you here." She gave Maya a look, which only made Maya blush more.

"Just pulling a little breakfast duty before practice," he said, still holding the tray. "How about we eat outside on the balcony? The view is ridiculous."

"That'd be great," Maya said. Of course, she thought, the view will be even more ridiculous with him in it. Travis slid open her balcony door with his free hand and went to set up outside.

Renee sat down beside her. "How did you sleep on your first night here?"

Maya nearly purred. "Can you please tell me what this bed is made out of? I've never slept so well in my life."

"I forget," Renee said. "Something endangered."

Maya laughed. Renee didn't. *Oh.* Maya thought it best to

just move on to another subject before she thought about that too hard.

"I'm going to need a good breakfast," Maya said. "I have a monster day of packing ahead of me. Could she have left in a bigger hurry?"

"This is all your stuff," Renee said.

"No, that's all my stuff." Maya pointed to two dinky suitcases and a tennis bag in the corner.

"I couldn't have you staying in an empty room," Renee said. "So I bought all this from her. The bed, the dresser, the TV . . ."

"You . . . bought all this?" Maya asked. "For me?"

"Well, not so much bought as gave her a bunch of dresses for it. Don't worry, they were all last season. And it's yours just until you post naked pictures of yourself on the Internet. Then it's the next girl's."

Maya was overwhelmed. What could she say?

"Breakfast is served," Travis said, returning. Maya got out of bed, but before she could go outside, she saw Nicole at her door.

"Are you guys still in your pajamas?" Nicole asked. She was in full tennis gear.

"The gang's all here!" Renee exclaimed. "Perfect time for our first roomie meal together."

"No can do," Nicole said. "I have court time at eight. Maya, I sacked my practice partner because he hit like a girl. You want to hit with me instead? You can keep up."

Did Nicole think she even had to ask? "Yeah, sure," Maya said without hesitation.

"Hey," Travis said. "I slaved hard over this meal. Okay, Butler slaved hard over this, but I had to carry it."

Maya lingered.

"Like, eight on the dot," Nicole said, looking at her Rolex. "Ticktock."

Maya didn't know what to do.

"Go." Travis sighed. "Renee and I will eat it."

"That's way too many calories," Renee said.

"I will eat it," Travis corrected. He really was something else.

Maya hugged him, grabbed her tennis clothes, and ran to the bathroom. Within three minutes, she and Nicole were out the door.

Maya had never walked a red carpet before, but she imagined it was a lot like walking to the tennis courts by Nicole's side. The adoration she got from passersby was epic.

"It's got to be an amazing feeling," Maya couldn't help but remark. "Everybody loves you."

"If I needed this much love and slobbering, I'd get a dog," Nicole said.

A guy in a suit approached. The amount of grease in his thinning hair was rivaled only by the amount of desperation in his eyes.

"Nicole," he said, "I'm a big fan. You're such a strong role model, especially for the Latina community. I manufacture my own chili sauce. You'd be a perfect spokesperson. A spicy girl for a spicy sauce, 'Serving up the *caliente* one bottle at a time!'"

Maya couldn't tell what was more offensive, the slogan or the fact that it was a middle-aged white guy saying it.

Nicole didn't break her stride. "You know what, I don't make any business decisions. My agent is waiting for me on the court. If you want to run ahead and tell her about this wonderful idea before I get there . . ."

He just stood there, ever hopeful.

"Run along," she said. Oh right, his expression seemed to say, that was his cue.

"Thank you, Nicole. It was great talking to you, Nicole." He started jogging ahead of them. "See you at the court, Nicole."

"'Serving up the *caliente* one bottle at a time'?" Maya repeated.

"I'm sure I'm in a sombrero somewhere strumming a guitar," Nicole said. "Or swinging a racket at a piñata."

Maya laughed. "Your agent is going to kill you for siccing him on her."

"Oh please, Jordan lives for this," Nicole said. "Some people need coffee to start their day. Jordan needs to bite the heads off morons and feast on their carcasses."

Nicole and Maya reached the court, which had its normal Nicole King crowd (including the greasy chili-sauce hawker, who waited on the other side of the fence angling for Jordan's attention). There was, however, a new face at the gate. And it just so happened to belong to the current hottest hip-hop artist in the game. So big that Maya completely blanked on his name.

"That's . . . isn't that . . . you know who I'm talking about . . . ," Maya said.

Security had given him the spot of honor by the gate so he could get a moment with Nicole.

"What up, girl," he said. "You gonna kill it today or what?" It was half question, half pick-up line.

Nicole smiled. "What do you think?" The words poured out of her slow like honey.

The crowd fed off their chemistry, snapping picture after picture.

"I think you gonna do what you do," he said, a sly grin spreading across his face.

"Maybe you should stick around and see," Nicole suggested.

"I think I will." He took out his phone, then pulled her in for a self-portrait. "This one's for Twitter, so make it hot."

"I always do." She smiled.

Nicole and Maya stepped onto the court, shut the gate, and headed to the bench.

"What a hack," Nicole said. "Plus, he's like, what, fifty? I'm seventeen. Pretty sure that'll get you a court date, dude. And I don't mean the tennis court."

"I don't get it," Maya said. "It looked like you were kind of, I don't know, feeling him."

"You may be good at tennis," Nicole said, "but you have a lot to learn about the game."

Maya looked on as Nicole met up with Jordan, who was never not on her cell.

"*Tonight Show* wants you for the eighteenth," Jordan said. "That's the same night as the Grammys. Nike's opening a store in Manhattan on the twenty-fourth, but you're in Barcelona for a tournament. And Turkish Airlines wants you for three commercials—they'll shoot wherever you want. Maui's nice this time of year."

Maya was dizzy just hearing all of it. She could only imagine how Nicole processed it.

"What dresses do we have for the Grammys?" Nicole asked, not missing a beat. "Who else is going to be on the show and at the opening, and do the airlines want print, too? If so, how many zeroes?"

"Balenciaga, Diane von Furstenberg, and Gucci," Jordan said. "Gyllenhaal, Lil Wayne on the show, Dwayne Wade at the store, no print, high six."

"Dwayne is dead sexy, hell yes on the store," Nicole said as she unzipped her bag and got her racket out. "Tell Barcelona I have a right hip flexor injury. No, shoulder, that way I can wear heels for Dwayne. And tell the airline they'll get one commercial, shot in . . . South Africa. I haven't been there in forever."

"What about the *Tonight Show* or the Grammys?" Jordan asked.

"Jake Gyllenhaal or Maggie Gyllenhaal?" Nicole asked, swigging water.

"Maggie," Jordan said.

"The Grammys," Nicole said. "I'd rather wear that Balenciaga." She turned to Maya, who was still hanging on *high six*. "Are we going to stand around yammering or are we gonna hit?"

Maya went back out on the court to battle Nicole. She managed to win a few points, but she was stretched even further past her own limit.

And she loved every minute of it.

Afterward, while Maya wiped herself down with a beach towel (once again, Nicole was dry as a bone), Nicole checked her cell phone.

"Good God, Renee," Nicole said, shaking her head.

"What's wrong?" Maya asked.

"Force of Habit is doing a private show tonight at the Sour. She was supposed to be my plus one for the after-party, but she just wants to hang at home."

"I love Force of Habit! They're my favorite band!" Maya blurted. She immediately heard what sounded like her begging and backed off. "I mean, who doesn't? Shouldn't be too hard to find someone else to go."

"Did you want to come?" Nicole asked. "Be my plus one?"

"I would love to," Maya said, leaping at the chance. And then it hit her. "Wait. I have plans already. My friend Cleo's coming over for a movie night." Cleo wasn't the only one coming over.

"Oh," Nicole said. "Too bad." And that was it.

"Well, I mean . . ." Maya couldn't let the offer slip away so fast. She needed time to think. Yes, Cleo wanted someone else there with her and Svetlana to keep it casual, but if Renee wasn't going out, she could play the third wheel. Maya wouldn't be stranding Cleo completely. "It'll be fine," she said finally. "We'll have plenty of movie nights. But Force of Habit is in town for one night only."

"Cool," Nicole said.

"Cool," Maya agreed.

.　.　.

The line to get into the Sour snaked from the bouncer all the way around the building. Maya approached it, decked out in a pair of Renee's Manolos (they were worth the bruises) and a ruffled silk Chloé dress that Renee said made her blue eyes pop out of her head like lasers. Renee also insisted she carry something called a Birkin bag, which was ridiculously large, especially considering all she had in it was her ID and a half-used lip balm. But it sure turned heads.

Of course, Maya's most head-turning accessory was one Miss Nicole King. In her silver Dior minidress and matching Jimmy Choos, she was turning it out. The world was Nicole's runway. And she could stomp it better than the models in Milan.

"You walk better in heels than in sneakers," Maya said.

"I play better in them, too." Nicole smiled.

As they got close enough, Maya spotted two things that made her nervous. The 21-and-over sign on the door and the fact that everyone in line had the same printed-out invitation they did.

"The line isn't moving at all," Maya said. "And they're carding. I don't have a fake ID."

"Don't worry about it," Nicole said. "You have a real me."

Nicole led Maya to the front of the line, passing a throng of paparazzi, who came to life upon seeing her. The only time the girls had to stop was for the bouncer to unhook the rope and open the door.

Inside the club was pure electricity. Actors and musicians mingled with supermodels and celebutantes. Maya felt like a spy as she studied them in their natural habitat. Without their guards up for the public, they were just as loud and silly as normal people. Except they were a million times richer.

Maya wondered what Cleo would think of this madness. She'd planned to wait for Cleo to show up at the villa tonight before leaving, but Nicole had insisted she couldn't hit this party without a decent pedicure. So she'd left her a note. Maya vowed to remember every little detail for her.

Maya surveyed the room and spotted another velvet rope. On the other side of it, she saw the guests of honor. Force of Habit! The entire band seemed to be doing shots with whoever brought them over. She could've stared at the band all night, but Nicole had other ideas. Before Maya knew it, she was at the bar having a drink poured for her.

The bartender smiled at Nicole as he handed her the drink. "I saw that picture you posted on Twitter. The real freaky one from the shower. Hilarious."

Maya froze.

"Thanks," Nicole said. She turned to Maya, who gripped her drink white-knuckled. After giving herself a perm in the sixth grade, posting that picture of Nicole online was Maya's biggest regret in life.

"Relax." Nicole sipped her drink. "It's fine." But it wasn't fine. Not totally.

"It was a crappy thing to do," Maya said, unwilling to be let off the hook.

"Yeah, it was," Nicole agreed. "But, you know, I did trick you into breaking and entering. . . ." It was the other elephant in the room.

"Sliding and entering," Maya said out of habit.

"What?" Nicole asked.

"That's what I said when Nails was chewing me out," Maya said. "I said I didn't actually break anything. I thought it was a good argument."

" 'Sliding and entering'?" A small smile crept across Nicole's face.

"You should have seen his face when I said it," Maya remembered. "He was like . . ." Maya made a face that was somewhere between horror and pity. Nicole smiled wider. "He already thought I was a moron. I mean, who does Cirque du Soleil through a window for a poster? That isn't even hers? And there I am pleading, 'I did it for the sick kid in the hospital!' "

Nicole laughed. "Sorry. I'm going to hell for that one. But did you see my thighs in that poster? And then you take that picture of me in the shower and put it on blast to, like, millions of people. . . ." Nicole laughed harder. Which made Maya laugh. "And people were like, 'Oh, you were so brave to post that, Nicole.' I almost had a benefit thrown in my honor!"

"We've been causing problems for each other since I got here," Maya said. "Meanwhile I'm doing nothing but trying to stay out of your way. . . ."

"And I'm thinking, who is this chick and why is she in my face, like, every minute?" Nicole kept laughing. "My car, my shower, my house . . . everywhere!"

"And I was thinking, when is this girl going to kill me?" Maya fought to get the words out, she was laughing so hard. "I had Cleo on night watch while I slept!"

They were each wiping tears from their eyes.

"You are one scary person," Maya finally said. "I don't know if anyone's ever told you that."

"Once or twice," she said. "I hope you're not scared of me anymore." Nicole handed her a napkin to wipe her mascara.

"As long as you're not trying to kill me in my sleep," Maya said.

"I make no promises." Nicole smiled. For the first time, Maya felt like they were really becoming friends. Nicole was no longer this untouchable idol. She was flesh and blood. And Maya liked her that way.

They continued exploring the party, making friends in every corner. And enjoying each other's company. Maya was a huge hit in her public debut, scoring appreciative looks from a whole bunch of guys. This time, when Nicole left her to say hi to random people and she was alone, she didn't feel terror like she had at the costume party. Here at the Sour, she'd never felt better.

It was at that exact moment when Maya was on her own and feeling fabulous that she was suddenly slammed into from behind. She looked down at her dress to find a vodka cranberry running down her.

"Hey!" She turned to the guy, who was just as annoyed at her.

Jeans, T-shirt. True to form, he couldn't be bothered to make an effort at all. Jake.

"I thought you had to have good vision to be a tennis player," Jake said.

"You bumped into me!" Maya yelled over the music. Though she probably didn't have to yell that loud. "How about an 'I'm sorry'? Or have you never said those words in your life?"

"Kitty has claws," Jake said, taking in her outfit. "How about we just kiss and make up?"

"There is nowhere on earth dark enough for that," Maya said, revolted. She looked at the stain. She'd been so happy to fit in, if just for a moment. Now she was back to looking like a fool.

"Here, I'll help you clean up." Jake grabbed a rag from the nearby bar and began wiping her down. Not only was he essentially pawing her, he was smearing the dirty rag on her, making it worse.

"Thanks, I've got it!" Maya said, snatching the rag away. She grabbed an unattended water bottle off the bar, soaked some napkins, and tried to mitigate the damage.

"Where's Travis tonight?" Jake asked.

"He has practice in the morning," she said. Travis had texted her earlier, and she wished even more now that he was here. "Don't you have practice, too? I seem to recall you losing a bet or something?"

"I said I'd be there," Jake quipped. "I never said I'd be sober."

Maya just rolled her eyes.

"Where's Mandy?" Maya asked.

"Mindy," Jake corrected. "She's studying for the bar." Maya looked at him cock-eyed. Jake just laughed. "Kidding. She's right over there, hooking up with some guy."

He motioned to the bar. Sure enough, there was Mindy, sucking face with a bouncer.

Maya was horrified. "That doesn't bother you?"

"Why should it bother me?" It was a genuine question.

"Because you two were together?" she said. "And now you're not?" His expression was blank. "And you have emotions?"

Jake furrowed his brow. "You read a lot of romance novels, huh?" It was another genuine question.

"Normal people invest a little something in who they hook up with," Maya informed him. "I don't know if you've heard."

Jake smirked. "So says the girl who made out with me in the dark at some random party."

"I thought you were Travis!" Maya said.

"Who you barely knew," Jake lobbed back at her. "That doesn't bother you? Don't you have emotions?"

Maya clenched. "That is not the same thing."

"No, you're right," Jake agreed. "I knew Mindy longer."

She was stymied. Jake was absolutely right. He was enjoying watching her squirm.

"What is your problem?" she asked. More like demanded.

"I don't have a problem," he said glibly.

"Yeah, you do," Maya shot back.

"Yeah?" Jake scratched his head. "What is it, then?"

"You," she said. "You're one big, walking problem. You're a brat, you say whatever comes to your head, you complain about everything even though you could have whatever you want, you have no respect for women, you're every girl's nightmare, you're just a terrible, terrible person."

Jake just looked at her. "Are you as turned on as I am?"

Maya was flabbergasted. Absolutely flabbergasted. "Enjoy

the rest of your evening, Jake. If you'll excuse me, I'm going to go enjoy mine."

With that, Maya fled, leaving Jake behind smiling.

Maya looked high and low for Nicole. She couldn't risk being alone anymore lest she get dragged into another ridiculous conversation. Finally, she found her. She was on the other side of the second velvet rope, making out with the Force of Habit lead singer.

Maya made her way over, trying to play it nonchalantly.

"Maya!" Nicole said, seeing her and unsuctioning herself from his lips. "You know Adam, right?"

Maya was too starstruck to speak. So she just nodded, which actually served to make her look cool and aloof.

"Nice to meet you, Maya," he said. He was beyond wasted, barely able to work out the mechanics of a handshake. He was also only a few years younger than the hip-hop guy Nicole mused could go to jail for flirting with her, but she didn't seem too concerned about the fate of this guy.

Nicole introduced her to the rest of the band, putting extra emphasis on the drummer. Then she pulled Maya in for a one-on-one.

"The drummer thinks you're hot," Nicole said. "They're staying at the Borealis."

"Um," Maya said. "I'm kinda dating Travis. . . ."

Nicole raised her eyebrows.

"I'm flattered, but . . . I think I'm okay." Maya wasn't sure what was more surreal, getting attention from the drummer of Force of Habit or being in any position to turn him down.

Nicole just turned to the drummer. "She's not interested. Sorry."

Maya was wide-eyed. How could Nicole just drop that on him so bluntly?!

"No, I'm . . . no offense," Maya said, her face so bright red that even Crayola couldn't replicate it. "It's not like you're not . . . I'm just . . . there's this guy . . ."

"That's cool," the drummer said without a hint of irritation. "I'll just go home with her." He motioned to the model across the table, who'd heard the whole thing and still smiled like she'd won the lottery.

Nicole looked at Maya as if to say, *See, not a big deal.* There was a lot to learn about how this other world operated, and Maya felt seriously behind the curve.

"Cool," Maya said.

Maya spent the next couple of hours partying with the band. Which really just amounted to listening to their stories and making them feel like they were kings of the universe. Which wasn't difficult, because, to Maya, they were.

"Hey," Adam said to Nicole as the night wound down. "Wanna blow out of here?"

Nicole smiled. "Maya?"

"Sure," Maya said. "I'm ready when you are." Maya was definitely ready to call it a night. Nicole's life was thrilling but exhausting. She could only really take a few hours at a time.

Maya, Nicole, and Adam made their way to the exit. When they stepped out onto the sidewalk, they were overwhelmed by a wall of light. The minute the paparazzi saw Nicole and Adam together, they went crazy.

"The limo's not here," Adam slurred.

The only means of escape was Nicole's car.

"Come on," Nicole said. They forced their way through the throngs of photographers and got to her Aston Martin. A two-seater. The photographers were circling them.

"It's okay," Maya said, doing the math. "Go."

Nicole gave her a look that was both thankful and apologetic, then jumped in the car and took off in a blur.

As the photographers chased after them trying to snag a few last shots, Maya dug into her borrowed Birkin to find that she'd spent the forty dollars she'd brought on two drinks. She had no money for a cab, and everyone she knew had already left.

Or almost everyone.

"Need a lift?"

Jake pulled up next to her in his black '68 Firebird. It had a gold phoenix that covered the entire hood. It was an odd choice for someone who could afford a way more expensive car, but everything about Jake was odd. Including the fact that there was no girl riding shotgun.

"I don't get in cars with people who've been drinking," Maya said.

"I didn't drink a drop. I have practice tomorrow," he said, smiling. "See, I'm not so terrible. Hop in."

"Aren't you saving that seat for someone with a higher skirt and lower standards?" Maya asked.

Jake grinned. "I copped all my feels in the bar, but it's nice to know you care."

Maya was taken aback, but she refused to show it. "I don't," she replied curtly.

"Don't what?" Jake said. "Need a ride, or care?"

"Both," she said.

"Really?" he said. "Because I can still smell the smoke from Nicole's tires."

"I'll take a cab," she huffed. "Cabs take credit cards." Then she remembered. She'd left her emergency credit card at home. She hadn't wanted to be tempted to use it at the bar and then have her father see on the statement where she'd spent her night. "Or IOUs . . ."

"You have no money on you?" Jake laughed. "Looks like you either hop in or walk home."

She was at his mercy. The fact that they both knew it only made her bristle more.

"It's a nice night," she said. "I'll take the walk."

"Suit yourself." With that, Jake sped off.

Alone again, she felt the immediate consequence of her decision staring her square in the face. It was four and a half miles back to the Academy. And there was no way she was doing this in heels.

Over an hour later, Maya arrived at the front gate. It was well past curfew; if she needed them to open the gate for her, she'd be reported immediately. She could've killed time for a few hours somewhere and strolled in with the sun, but how in the world would she explain the outfit to the guard? *Oh, don't mind me*, she imagined herself saying. *I simply can't go for my morning run without my heels and couture.* The only thing to do was jump the wall.

Jumping the wall would've been impossible for mere

mortals. But Maya was no mortal. She was tall. She was fit. Within five minutes . . . she was flat on her back in a bush.

As she struggled up out of the bushes, a flashlight trained on her face. It was a security guard. And not just any guard—he was the one who'd woken her up and carted her to Nails's office. As fast as she recognized him, he recognized her.

"I know you," he said. A smile crept onto his face.

It was official. She was screwed.

The guard escorted her to his nearby booth. He reached inside, removed something from a pile of papers, and promptly handed it to her. "This is you, right?"

It was the Academy welcome packet.

Maya didn't know how to respond. This is what he recognized her from? "Uh. Yeah . . ."

"I thought so," he said. "You must've been out late tonight. Looking like that, I bet it was a pretty fancy party."

If she didn't know any better, he almost sounded star-struck. Over her.

"It was," she said. "It was this after-party thing for a band." She didn't know why, but she felt compelled to be just a little more fabulous.

"Nice," he said, opening the gate . . . and ushering her in. "Have a good night."

That was it? She was off the hook, just like that? Maya wasn't going to let her own bafflement over this free pass keep her from darting inside that gate, so in she ran.

Once inside, she smiled, then she made her way back to the villa before he could change his mind.

Maya couldn't believe it. All this time she'd seen people

morph into fawning fools over Nicole. She'd witnessed all the perks that came with being put on a pedestal. But she'd never known what it was like to be on the receiving end of it. How she'd gotten to this place was thoroughly confusing, but Maya knew one thing for sure: it was like nothing she'd ever experienced in her life.

Chapter 14

Maya was passed out facedown on her bed still in her dress and heels. Somewhere in the deep recesses of her subconscious, she heard the faint sound of a phone ringing. It persisted, getting louder and louder, until it wrenched her from a sleep so deep she felt her body was still in it.

Her cell phone was blowing up.

Through the slit of a barely open eye, she read her screen. Missed texts, missed calls, a whole bunch of voice mails. One was even from her mother. What was going on?

She listened to her messages, each one making less sense in her haze than the one before. When she got to her mother's, she heard a few words strung together that made her sit bolt upright.

"Sweetheart, what's the Wall and why are you on it?"

The Wall was a major gossip site for celebrities and the people who lived vicariously through them. If you were on it, you were either sporting a baby bump, going into rehab, or wearing the fugliest dress known to man.

Maya grabbed her laptop and banged out the address.

There she was.

The item was mostly about Nicole and Adam, but Maya was in one of the pictures. She looked so glamorous, like a celebrity (the wonders of a cute dress and some makeup, she thought). And she was identified by name! The whole thing was so beyond cool that she felt like eight shots of espresso had suddenly surged through her veins. Tired? Who was tired? Despite getting three hours of sleep, she bounded from bed and got ready for class. The Wall!

The bounce in Maya's step carried her out of the villa and onto the quad. As she made her way to class, everything and everyone around her just seemed brighter. Friendlier. It was like she was in a musical or something. The more smiles she got, the more she realized—they were specifically for her. Everyone had seen the Wall, and they wanted her to know it.

Smiles became thumbs-ups. Thumbs-ups became winks. She couldn't help but smile back. This was a drug, and she wanted hit after hit after hit.

She took out her cell phone and looked at the picture for another little kick. Suddenly, something caught her eye. Something she hadn't noticed before. Something that stopped her dead in her tracks. Jake, who was standing next to her in the picture, was referred to in the caption as her date.

Oh no, she thought, the blood rushing from her head. *Oh no no no no no no no no no.*

Was that what she was getting all these thumbs-ups for? All these winks and smiles? People thought that she was . . . that they were . . . ?

Just then, she saw him. Jake. He was beelining right for her.

"Don't you dare," Maya commanded as he got close. "I don't want to hear a single joke come out of your mouth. Not one."

But he was as heated as she was. "You think I think this is funny?"

"Oh, I think you think this is hilarious," she said. "In fact, I wouldn't put it past you to have planted it just to get a rise out of me."

"Someone thinks pretty highly of herself," Jake said. "What do you think this does for my dating life? Girls are going to think I've got a girlfriend."

Maya snorted. "I'm pretty sure the girls you hook up with don't care if you already have a girlfriend."

Maya's thoughts began to race. *What if Travis sees this? What if he already saw it? What if he thought it was true?* Each thought was like a terrible domino falling into the next.

"I'm breaking up with you," Jake said.

"What?" Maya asked.

"I said I'm breaking up with you, Maya!" He wasn't saying it to her. He was saying it to everyone in earshot. "It's over!"

How dare he, Maya thought. *He is breaking up with me? Is that what he wants people to think?* As she looked around, she saw he had not only gotten some people's attention, but they also seemed to be buying what he was saying. It made her furious.

"You can't break up with me!" Maya yelled. "We were never together in the first place!"

Jake refused to back down, making their scene even bigger. "I know I hurt you, Maya, but you have to move on!"

This guy was unreal.

Maya yelled even louder. "Move on?! The only thing bigger than your mouth is your ego!"

There were snickers and a smattering of applause. It only fueled them more. And Maya especially.

"Someday you'll see this breakup was for the best!" he yelled.

"Someday you'll be hit by a bus and I'll be the one at the wheel!" With that, Maya turned on her heel and stormed off. Behind her, she heard a wave of whistling and applause. The people had crowned a winner, and Maya couldn't help but enjoy it.

On her way to class, Maya managed to get a hold of Travis. He had seen the Wall and the bit about Jake, but the only thing he was upset about was missing out on seeing her in that dress. It allowed her to calm down.

"Last night was surreal," Maya told Cleo. "One minute Nicole, Adam, and I are walking out of the Sour, the next we're being chased like dogs across the parking lot. Nicole throws him in her car and tears off all *Fast and Furious*, I'm left choking on burnt rubber with no money and no way home—"

"Dogs chase," Cleo said plainly.

"What?" Maya asked, interrupted.

"You said you were chased like dogs, but dogs are the ones that chase. The photographers would be the dogs." Cleo lazily flipped a page in her textbook.

"Okay, fine, they were dogs," Maya said, continuing. "So then Jake pulls up in his stupid car and you would not believe what he had the nerve to say to me. . . ."

"Sounds like a crazy night," Cleo said.

"Is everything okay?" Maya asked.

"What happened to you last night?" Cleo asked finally. "You were supposed to be there with me and Svetlana."

"I'm sorry," Maya said, and it was genuine. "I will definitely be there next time, I promise. Going to that after-party was just a once-in-a-lifetime opportunity."

"You've been having a lot of those lately," Cleo said rather flatly.

"I know, right?" Maya smiled.

Mr. Manjarrez made his way to the back of the class. He was dropping essays on each student's desk along the way. When he arrived at Maya's, he had nothing.

Maya realized. She never wrote her essay. She didn't even remember what it was supposed to be about.

"The Bay of Pigs," he said, as if reading her mind.

As he stood there, Maya suddenly had the same feeling of being screwed that she had last night (this morning?) with the security guard. Which gave her an idea. If a little stardust could help get her out of that jam, maybe it could get her out of this one, too. It was a ridiculous idea. Crazy, even. But she had no other choice, so she just went for it.

"Mr. Manjarrez," Maya said, "I'm really sorry. I typed the deadline into my calendar, but it's not there anymore. . . ." She waved her phone, knowing full well her glamour shot on the Wall was still on it.

He took the phone and looked at the picture. Here she was on this amazing site, looking like a full-blown star. He scanned the rest of the photos, a wry smile spreading on his face. "Partying a little too hard with Nicole King and one of the Reed boys, I see."

"I guess . . . ," Maya said. She couldn't help but wonder if that was a good thing or a bad thing.

Finally, he handed Maya back her phone. "I suppose I could give you an extension. Take another couple of days to finish."

"Thank you," Maya said gratefully as he walked on.

"What was that?" Cleo asked.

"What?" Maya replied innocently.

"If you hurled those pictures at him any harder, he would've gotten a concussion," Cleo said.

Maya focused on exiting out of the site and putting her phone away. "I needed a few extra days to write my paper and got them. It's no big deal."

" 'No big deal'?" Cleo asked. "Oh. Okay. No big deal. So, you're ready to dump that makeover, then, right?"

Maya hesitated. "I think I'm going to hold on to the whole makeover thing a little longer. But not out of vanity or anything. For the advantage."

" 'For the advantage'?" Cleo repeated.

"Look, Cleo," Maya said. "This place is about more than what you can do on a court or a field. Image matters. And for whatever reason, don't ask me why, this drag I'm in is worth something. Everyone has advantages here. Some kids are rich, some are connected. This is mine."

Cleo just looked at her. Maya read her face.

"Would you relax?" Maya said. "I'm just thinking smarter. I'm still the same person inside."

Just then, Mr. Manjarrez handed Cleo her paper back. On the top, in red: D.

Cleo freaked. "A D?! I can't get a D! I have to maintain at least a C average for my scholarship. I'll have to move into the library for the rest of the semester to bring my average back up!"

He was far from moved.

"Mr. Manjarrez," Maya said, intervening. "If Cleo turned in a crappy paper, it's all my fault. She shouldn't be punished for that. Could she, maybe, get a few extra days, too? To rewrite it?"

He considered it. He looked around to make sure none of the other kids in the class were paying attention, then gave a silent nod. He moved on.

Cleo was dumbfounded. Maya was smiling.

"See?" Maya said, vindicated. She'd proved her point, doing something nice for a friend. "It's all good."

The look on Cleo's face said a lot of things. And "all good" wasn't one of them.

Chapter 15

"So, was Travis pissed about the whole Jake thing on the Wall?" Nicole asked as she sprayed sunblock on her legs. It was a hot, steamy day, and she, Maya, and Renee were spending it on the sideline of the football field watching the guys practice.

"Not at all," Maya said. "I thought I was going to have to do all this explaining, but he was the one who kept apologizing to me."

"Why?" Renee asked. Maya's eyes were on Travis, but Renee's were on every other guy on the field.

"He was worried about my reputation," Maya said. "He said being associated with Jake in that way could be social suicide. Can't say I disagree."

"Jake really is not discriminating in the least," Renee said, ogling the entire defensive line.

Maya watched Travis avoid a tackle while managing to find an open man for a touchdown.

"Travis definitely got his dad's brain for strategy," Maya noticed.

"The only thing I know about football," Renee said as she continued to leer, "is that it gives you incredible thighs."

Nicole and Maya shared a laugh.

Maya continued to melt in the heat. Their umbrellas were useless. "There's more shade over there," Maya said. "Should we move?"

"Travis sat us here for a reason," Nicole said, spraying her body with tanner.

"What reason?" Maya asked.

Nicole gave Renee a pointed look.

"Why is this spot so special?" Maya asked. "What do you know?"

Renee smiled. "This is where the girlfriends sit."

Maya was awestruck by that. "The . . . ?"

Nicole and Renee drew closer to her. Gossip was a sport all its own here. A better sport.

"Are you official?" Nicole asked.

"No," Maya said. "I don't think so." She thought harder. "Maybe?" Finally, she was sure. "No. Not that we talked about." But where Travis sat her certainly tipped to his intentions.

"Would you want to be?" Renee asked.

"Maybe," she said. But there was no maybe about it.

A yell came from the field. The girls looked over. It'd come from Jake, who'd just successfully mauled another kid.

"Jake seems more wound up and bloodthirsty than usual," Maya noted.

"How can you even tell?" Renee asked, sliding a pickle from a plastic bag and giving it a munch.

Nicole looked at Renee. "Are you pregnant?"

"It's all I'm eating," Renee said. "The pickle diet is supposed to totally work."

"Renee," Nicole said.

"I'm telling you," Renee insisted. "It worked for my friend Angela's cousin Georgia's coworker Melissa."

Before Maya and Nicole could argue, there was another scream from the field. Except this one sounded primal, like a wounded animal. The girls looked over to see the guys all clustered together in chaos. Someone had been hurt. Badly.

Maya overheard one word muttered by a girl nearby, and it froze her: *quarterback*.

"Travis," Maya said under her breath. Before even she knew it, she was up like a flash. She ran to the field, Renee and Nicole following behind.

Maya's eyes searched for Travis, but she couldn't see him anywhere. Finally, she found him. He was totally fine, just one of the many in the cluster. Confused, Maya looked at what they were all huddled around. It was the other quarterback, writhing on the ground. With Jake standing over him. Jake had sacked him so hard that he'd broken the quarterback's arm.

Maya looked back to Travis, who looked at her. She could see it all over his face. This was not good.

·   ·   ·

Maya sat outside Nails's office yet again—this time with Travis and Jake. The door was closed, and Nails was on the other side of it having a conference with the injured QB's parents. She couldn't hear what was being said, but the intensity coming through the walls was loud and clear. For once, Nails was in the defensive position, and there was nothing he could do about it.

As the parents' voices rose, Maya studied Jake. He didn't seem to be registering any of it. He was bottled up, shut down. Gone.

"You went at him too hard," Travis told him. "You didn't have to go at him that hard."

Jake clearly didn't want to hear it. He didn't want to hear anything.

But they all snapped to attention when the door opened.

The kid's parents stormed out of the room. They blew past Travis and Maya, but they lingered at Jake. Their disgust at him was absolutely unmistakable. Maya was pretty sure the father wanted to go at him right then and there, but luckily the mother took his arm and walked him out.

Their anger paled in comparison to Nails's. When he walked out of his office and found Jake, he was at a pure boil.

"They're suing the Academy," Nails said. "They're coming after us, hard. That boy was being scouted by six different teams. You may have ended his career before it's begun."

"You get injured on the field," Jake finally said, defending himself. "It's sports, people get hurt. That's the risk you take when you go out there. The Academy can't be sued for that."

"No"—Nails stepped closer—"not unless there's a history

of unnecessary roughness, which you have. You're a disaster, I knew you were a disaster, and I let you stay out there. I let you stay on that field and now I'm being sued because of it." Nails was fired up. "I'm tired. Tired of being disappointed by you, tired of your constant screwing up. Why can't you be more like Travis?"

Maya felt like a massive interloper. She wanted to leave, badly. But she was trapped there. Trapped watching Nails take his son apart piece by piece.

"I've been stuck with the thankless job of taking care of you on my own," Nails said. "Considering your behavior around here, it's no wonder your mother isn't rushing back."

Just as Nails said this, Jake and Maya found each other's eyes. The pain was almost physical. Certainly worse than anything the kid he injured was feeling.

Travis wasn't intervening. Perhaps this was a scene that had played out so much that Travis was used to it. Or maybe there was no stopping Nails when he was on a roll. Either way, in this moment, Jake was totally alone. And Maya saw that in his eyes, too.

"You're an embarrassment," Nails said. "I can't even look at you. Go."

Without a word, Jake stalked off. He slammed the door so hard behind him that it swung back open and took a doorknob-sized chunk out of the wall.

Travis immediately went to his dad's side.

"It doesn't do anyone any good getting worked up like this," Travis said. "It'll be okay."

It was tough for Maya to tell if Travis was taking sides or if this was just his role in the Reed family psychodrama.

The more she thought about it, the more she didn't care. She couldn't help but stay on Jake. On the wounded animal she saw behind his eyes.

As Travis continued to soothe his father, Maya found herself slipping out, unnoticed.

Maya had absolutely no idea what she was doing there, but she was standing outside Jake's door. She had just felt compelled to follow him here.

The door was ajar. She knocked lightly. It would be so easy to turn around and leave. So why wasn't she? She knocked again, which only made the door open a little more. She heard Jake inside.

She let herself in.

Jake's place was massive. It was also barren. There were no decorations, no plants, no anything that would imply that someone rich lived there. Or anyone at all. The sole piece of furniture in the entire place was an old leather couch. It's where Jake sat. Crying.

Maya was frozen. She'd never seen Jake weak. Or vulnerable in any way. She knew he was upset back in Nails's office, but she had no idea just how much he was holding in, or how good he was at it.

It was at that very moment when Jake looked over. She tensed. But he was too upset—or defeated—to question her being there.

"Travis is the golden child . . . ," Jake said, talking at the floor. "He's always been the golden child. Travis is the smart one, the star. And I'm garbage."

Maya stayed back, like he was a lion that could strike at any moment.

"The only one who never treated me like a mistake was my mom," he said. It was like his face was using up all the emotion and there was none left for his voice. "But she took off because she couldn't take my father anymore. He's an American hero. He's God's gift to Astroturf. And he cheats on my mother like it's his job."

The tears kept streaming down his face. He wiped them, but it was useless.

"She knows he cheats on her," he said. "She acts like she doesn't, but she does. She couldn't take it, so she left. First it was for a week, then a month. It's been half a year. My father drove her away, and now I have no one."

Maya stepped closer, as if her body was acting independently from her will.

"Only you can know how crappy that feels," Maya said, empathizing. "But I know how big this place is when you feel like you have no one. And you're treated like a no one."

He looked at her for the first time.

She continued. "Pretty soon your mind starts tricking you into believing it. But you're not a no one, Jake. You're not a no one."

Suddenly, Jake cracked. He went from sad . . . to scared.

"I didn't mean to hurt him," Jake said desperately. "I swear, I didn't mean to hurt that kid. I don't know what happened.

Sometimes I get so angry I don't see . . . I can't . . . I feel so bad. I feel so bad."

She sat down next to him, though it was more like her legs gave out from under her and she ended up on the couch.

"I know," Maya said. "I know you do."

They were close. Nearly touching.

Jake leaned in and kissed her. But this time, it was no mistake. This time it was for real. And it was intense. Maya kissed him back harder. As he pulled her completely onto the couch, she realized. She didn't hate him. She didn't even sort of dislike him. This whole time, all she really wanted was this. And from what she could tell, that's all he'd wanted to do, too.

She kissed him some more. Despite the fact that this was not her normal, despite the fact that she'd never done this with anyone, Maya took off his shirt. And she let him take off hers.

Suddenly, Maya saw what she was doing. She backed off on the couch.

"No," she said, out of breath. "I don't know . . . I don't know where this is . . . going, but if it's where I think you think this is going . . ."

"I don't think this is going anywhere," he said, equally flushed.

"I just . . . I've never gone . . . there before," she said. "I'm not ready, I'm . . ." She suddenly felt like a geek. Or a freak. Or whatever the worse one was. She was with a guy who'd notched so many marks in his bedposts they looked like toothpicks. And here she was, this frigid girl who couldn't give him what she was sure he wanted, what everyone else did.

Jake just smiled.

"This is definitely good enough," he said.

And, looking in his eyes, she knew he was telling the truth.

Maya smiled. She kissed him. And they got right back to making out. For three hours, it was definitely, definitely good enough.

Chapter 16

Even though it was barely 8:00 a.m., it was somehow even steamier than it had been yesterday. Maya stood at the edge of the Academy's Olympic-sized swimming pool watching Renee do laps. She'd promised Renee she'd help get her time up, but since she didn't know much about swimming, that meant she would be on stopwatch duty.

But as she stared at the numbers, all Maya saw was Jake. And Jake's couch. And her on them both.

What did she know about him, really? Jake was as unstable as Travis was reliable. He was as raw as Travis was refined. Jake fought everyone and everything, including and especially himself, while Travis accomplished every goal without breaking a sweat. Getting caught up in your emotions made you vulnerable on the tennis court. Weak. Was she sabotaging herself off the court as well? Had she been fearless and true to herself last night, or self-destructive and reckless?

"There you are," Nicole said, finding her. "We're going to the beach."

"We are?" Maya asked. "When?"

"As soon as you can put on a bathing suit," Nicole said. "It's going to be a thousand degrees out today, and I'm not spending it sucking face with an air conditioner."

Renee bobbed her head above water just long enough to see Nicole. She started paddling her way over to say hi.

"I have class," Maya said. "And practice."

Nicole was less than impressed. "School and practice will be there tomorrow. And the next day, and the day after that, and the day after that . . ."

"Plus, Renee's been desperate to cut her lap time," Maya told her, reinforcing her case. "And I said I'd be here to work the stopwatch."

"There's a pace clock right there," Nicole said. Sure enough, there it was, hanging over the pool. "No sense in you roasting on the sidelines."

"What's up?" Renee said, finally making her way over.

"Maya wants to go to the beach, but she doesn't want to hurt your feelings," Nicole said.

"No," Maya said. "I said I'd be here for moral support and I will be. I want to be."

"It's okay if you want to go," Renee said. "I'm going to be here all morning. And you have been a little distracted."

Maya tensed.

"Distracted by what?" Nicole asked.

"Nothing, I . . ." Maya didn't know what to say.

Nicole was already over it. "Come on, Maya, let's go."

Maya had to admit to herself that being there—or anywhere on campus, where Jake was roaming free—was enough to drive her insane. Still, she could tell Renee really wouldn't mind if Maya stayed.

"I'll make it up to you," Maya said.

"Sure," Renee said, offering a smile.

With that, Nicole dragged a far-from-unwilling Maya away.

Nicole and Maya worked on their tans. The sound of the ocean beat the sound of chalk on a blackboard any day. Not that much ocean could be heard above the sounds of laughter and everyone's stereos battling for attention. The beach was cracking.

"I'm not sad to be missing class," Maya said. "I do feel a little guilty about missing practice, though."

"Practice, schmactice," Nicole said. "Listen, I was playing the quarterfinals of the Australian Open last year. A hundred degrees out, on-court temperature a hundred thirty. No roof, no third-set tiebreak, after four hours I was straight-up hallucinating. I thought my tennis bag was talking to me. But because I put in the time here getting used to the conditions, I pulled that one out. I lived to fight another day."

"So what you're saying is, going to the beach is part of a winning training regimen?" Maya asked.

Nicole smiled. "And you were afraid you wouldn't learn anything today. Pass me an *Us Weekly*."

Maya turned to their stack of magazines. Just in time to see Travis and Jake walking toward them. "What are they doing here?"

"I invited them," Nicole said. "I hope that was okay."

"Of course," Maya said quickly. Maybe too quickly.

"Ladies," Travis said as they arrived. Before Maya could say a word, Travis kissed her hello. If there was a Guinness World Record for least amount of time it took before things got awkward, she broke it right here.

"Hi," Maya managed. She met Jake's eyes. It was clear neither of them had made any move to share with anyone what went down last night. This wouldn't be the place to start.

"That bathing suit is definitely *bam*," Travis said, putting his arm around her. By the looks Jake was sneaking, the feeling was shared. Maya didn't know what to do or how to act. But she needed to put the kibosh on any PDA before it got weird.

"I should put a T-shirt on," Maya said. "The sun is so strong, I don't want skin cancer. . . ." She moved away from his arm and went to grab her top.

"Nah," Travis said. "You just need more sunscreen. Here, I'll put some on you." Travis got the bottle. "Lie down."

Maya's eyes widened. "I heard too much sunscreen was bad for you, too," she said in a panic. *Great*. And now she looked suspicious. "Ha," Maya forced a laugh. "Just kidding." No choice, she lay on her stomach. As Travis popped open the bottle and began putting more sunscreen on her, it officially went from awkward to beyond awkward.

Jake did his best to play it off, but this was obviously painful for him to watch.

"I'm surprised you can be so calm about it, Jake," Nicole said. "After what happened yesterday."

Jake looked at Nicole, completely rigid. "What are you talking about?"

Maya was even more rigid.

"Well, the Academy is being sued," Nicole went on. "I heard Nails laid into you pretty bad."

Jake turned to Travis and Maya. Travis immediately went on the defense.

"I didn't tell a soul," Travis said.

"Me neither," Maya said.

"I didn't hear it from them," Nicole said. "Word travels fast, remember."

"Wow. Yeah. Well." It was all Jake could say.

"Things happen," Travis said. "People get caught up in the moment. They do things."

Was he talking about Nails? Jake? Or her and Jake?

"You learn from your mistakes and you move on," Travis continued. "You hope to, anyway."

"Of course," Nicole said. "That quarterback will learn not to hold on to the ball so damn long."

They all looked at her.

"Oh, whatever, you were all thinking it," Nicole said. Then she held out a bottle to Jake. "I could use more sunscreen, too." She lay down on the blanket.

Maya watched him awkwardly take the bottle.

"This is tanning lotion," Jake said, hesitating. Maya could tell he didn't want to rub down Nicole in front of Maya any more than she wanted Travis to rub her down in front of him.

"Same diff," Nicole replied. She untied her bikini strings and let them fall over her shoulders.

Seemingly against his will, Jake put lotion on Nicole. It was Maya's turn to squirm.

"Where did you go last night, Maya?" Travis asked. "I turned around in the office after that whole . . . thing . . . and you were gone."

"Um," Maya said. "It was a little intense in there. Like a family thing. I figured I should just kind of leave you to it." Maya was pleased. She might have just made her first good lie.

"I called you," Travis said. "You never called me back."

"Uh . . ." Maya went blank. Her triumph was short-lived. She suddenly realized she hadn't seen her phone since last night.

"I found your phone," Jake said. He pulled it out of his pocket and handed it back to her. "You dropped it."

"Right," Maya said, red-faced. "Thanks." She took it back like contraband and shoved it in her bag. They both knew where she'd dropped it. She couldn't believe she could be so careless.

"Where did you drop it?" Travis asked.

"The field," Maya said.

"The office," Jake said at the exact same time.

"Between the field and the office," Jake said. He was clearly better at lying than Maya was.

"Didn't we get to the office before Maya?" Travis asked his brother.

Maya's eyes darted back to Jake.

"I went back to the field after I left the office," Jake said. "I needed to run drills, get that whole thing out of my system."

Jake was better than she'd thought. Scarily better.

As quick as Jake was, though, Travis was quicker. He gave Jake a sideways glance. "Want to go for a walk?" Travis asked Maya.

"Sure," she said. Travis helped her up. She and Jake exchanged a glance as Travis led her away.

Maya and Travis stood under the pier, the ocean lapping at their feet. There really was nothing more picture-perfect than the light reflecting off the water. But Travis was just looking at Maya.

"It's crazy the way things turn out," he said finally. "I invited you to come watch my practice, and the day winds up like that. . . ."

If he only knew, Maya thought.

"I bet that poor quarterback is thinking the same thing," she said. "It's so easy to get hurt at the Academy. Doing what we do." She was talking about sports. At first, anyway. "It's so easy to hurt someone when . . . when that's the last thing you want to do."

Maya wasn't sure who was getting hurt, Travis or Jake. Most likely all three of them.

Travis smiled. "You're amazing."

If she was so amazing, why did she feel so completely dysfunctional?

"I know we haven't really talked about, you know, us," he said. "Where we're at and stuff. But . . . I was hoping that where I sat you at practice might've given you a clue how I feel. What I want with you."

She looked at him. Was he really going to say what she thought he was going to say? Of all the times, right here, right now?

"I want you to be my girlfriend," he said. "I want to be your boyfriend. Just you and me. Exclusive."

Her brain locked. She'd dreamed of this moment since the day she walked on campus. More like fantasized, because she never thought it could be physically possible. But here she was, this was happening. So why couldn't she open her mouth?

He pushed on.

"You've got everything," he said. "You're gorgeous. You're sweet. People at the Academy look up to you. And we make a great team. It wouldn't just be the Academy we'd take over."

She looked at him. *Take over?*

"I've got plans, Maya," he continued. "I know how this works. Just by linking up, we become a story for people. A soap opera to follow. They'll give us a nickname like Traya or Mavis. We'll start popping up on the Wall every day. We won't have to go where the paparazzi's at; they'll come to us. We'll transcend sports and crack the mainstream. We'll be celebrities. You think you can imagine what being part of an It couple is like, but you have no idea. Everyone is going to know who you are. Everyone. You won't experience a life you've only ever dreamed about. You'll experience one you never knew existed. All this, just by saying yes."

Maya was overwhelmed.

"You're doing it again," she was finally able to say.

"Doing what?" he asked.

"The grand-gesture thing."

"Okay, sue me," he said. "Maya, I want to give you the world."

"Why," she asked, "does it feel like you want to give me to the world?"

"What are you talking about?"

"Travis, it's just . . ." Maya struggled to find the words. "First you woo me without even knowing me and now you want to take this show on the road before we're even together. It's all a big performance with you, and I don't even know where I am in all of this. Me, Maya. You may someday have these big feelings for me, but . . ."

Travis's face was blank. The truth is, she didn't know what she was getting at, either. Not totally. But she had an answer to his original question. And when she said it, it felt like the words were coming out of someone else's lips.

"I think you're amazing, too," Maya said. "And I do have feelings for you, but . . ." There was no other way to say it. "I have feelings for someone else, too." She could feel Travis stiffen, but if she didn't get this out now she never would. "And the feelings I have for him are . . . They're too strong for me to make any kind of commitment to you. Not the one you're asking for. It wouldn't be fair. Not to him, and not to you."

His face, always so pleasant and sure, darkened.

"Jake," he said. "That's who you're talking about, who you have these feelings for. It's Jake."

Her breath caught in her chest. All she could do . . . was nod.

"Unreal." He repeated the word over and over, reality sinking in deeper and deeper each time. "You're telling me, right here, that you have a choice between me and Jake and you're picking Jake?"

"I'm not picking anyone. All I said was—"

"I'm the one you should be with," he said, beginning to seethe. "Not him. I'm the one with the future. I'm the one with the heat."

"Travis, nobody said . . ." But Maya wasn't getting any words out with Travis this intense. And he was more intense than she'd ever seen him.

"Maya, if you want to be a someone, you need to be *with* a someone. I'm a someone." Travis met her eyes with a sharp focus. "No one is going to care if you're with Jake. I'm the one that people care about. I'm the one you should care about."

This was a side of Travis she didn't know existed. A side that to this point he'd kept expertly hidden. He was an egomaniac. It wasn't a good look. Still, she could see he was hurt. And she was the one who'd hurt him. Finally, she said the only thing she could think to say.

"I'm sorry." Maya moved closer, but Travis just walked off. "Travis!"

He was gone.

Before she could fully digest what had just happened, she saw someone nearby, watching from behind one of the columns of the pier.

"Jake."

His face said . . . she didn't know what it said. And the fact that she couldn't figure it out undid her.

"How much . . . how much did you hear?" Maya asked.

"Everything," he said. "The whole . . . everything."

The fact that Jake wasn't rushing into her arms told Maya all she needed to know. There was something between them. But "something" and hearing a girl create a movie-worthy romance where there wasn't one was "something" else entirely. She felt like a fool.

"Okay," she said, backpedaling. "I said I had feelings for you. And maybe I do. But that's all they are. Feelings. I don't expect anything from you. I know feelings aren't really your thing, at least with just one girl, and you certainly don't have to feel the same way about me. . . ."

This was where, if he did have any feelings for her, he would cut her off. He would put her out of her misery, sweep her up in his arms, and, as the music swelled and the cool water lapped at their feet, tell her he felt the same way she did. This is where that would happen. But he just stood there, silent.

"I'm sorry," he said finally.

Oh no. This had just happened. This exact thing. Except she was Travis and Jake was her. And it sucked being on the Travis side of things.

"I'm just . . . blown away," he said: "Seeing myself win out over Travis, for anything . . . I've just never been here before." He wasn't rejecting her. He was stunned.

"You're . . . not freaked out?" she asked.

He smiled.

"I'm not freaked out at all," he said. Then he stepped closer, grabbed her face, and kissed her. Hard.

"Would it freak you out if I gave you this?" he asked. He gripped his chain, where his dog tag hung.

"I've never seen you without that," she said.

"First time for everything," he replied. For all the grand gestures his brother threw at her, this small, simple thing landed with a boom.

"I may not be the smartest guy," he said, "I may be a punk, I may not do the right thing all the time. But I don't lie. I don't say things to get away with anything or get my way. What I do and what I say, you can trust. So trust me right now. I'm scared as hell. But I know I want you to have this."

He took her breath away. She thought that she knew Travis this whole time and that she didn't know Jake at all. But it was the other way around. From day one, she and Jake were real jerks with each other. *They were real.*

She smiled. "No," she said finally. "You giving me this wouldn't freak me out at all."

He took his chain off, then put it around her neck. It was more valuable than anything she'd ever borrowed from Renee.

"Wow," Maya said, taking it in. "A girl in a bikini and a dog tag . . . that's kind of hot."

Jake nodded. "Yes, it is."

Earlier, Maya had thought she wasn't ready to make a commitment under that pier, but she was wrong. She was ready to make one after all.

"So what's our couple name?" Maya asked. "Make? Jaya?"

" 'Couple name'? That's the stupidest thing I've ever heard in my life." He laughed. So did she.

They went back to kissing and didn't stop, even after Nicole packed up the car and left.

Chapter 17

Maya went for a quick morning run around the Academy. That was the intention, anyway, but since it took her forever now to get ready in the mornings, it wound up being a few laps around the parking lot. Far less impressive, but she looked great doing it.

Throughout her laps, Jake's dog tag kept bouncing up and hitting her in the face. But she suffered it gladly. It was her favorite accessory. Maya had always wondered what type of guy she'd end up with, and Jake was light-years away from who she'd imagined: a rich kid with anger issues, a car with a thunderbird on the hood, and the kind of mouth you wanted to wash out with soap, after giving it a good slap. And she loved it.

Wait. Did she love him? Was that the same? Was she *in love* with him? How would she know?

Her mind was racing when she arrived back at the villa . . . and found Jake waiting for her on the front steps.

"Well, hello, there," Maya said, smiling. "Isn't this a little early for you to be up?"

"Haven't gone to bed yet," he said, pulling her in for a kiss. She'd been fighting him so long that freely kissing him—and out in the open—still felt wrong. But it also made it that much more exciting.

"I already ate breakfast," she said. "But I can make you a shake or something if you're hungry."

"I can't stay," he said. "I've got some big news. I wanted you to hear it from me first."

"You've been offered an Armani underwear campaign," she guessed. "No, you're being drafted by the New England Patriots. No, underwear."

"If you want to see me in my underwear, all you have to do is ask," he smirked.

She gave him a warning look. "Jake . . ." When he smiled, she did, too. She was so easy to mess with.

"This news isn't about me," he said. "It's about you."

"About me?" Maya couldn't even make a joke guess. What kind of news would Jake have about her?

"You know how colleges and Olympic teams recruit from the Academy," he said.

"Yeah . . . ?"

"Well, so does Hollywood," he said. "Anytime they need someone who can play a sport on camera, they come here. There's a director who needs someone who can play tennis in his next movie. And . . ." He paused for effect. "You're one of the few girls the Academy's flying out to audition."

She just looked at him. "You're such a liar. Me, trying out

for a movie." She wasn't going to fall for any more of his she-nanigans.

"If you don't believe me, ask my dad," he said.

She eyed him. "Your dad . . . ?" After their big blowout, Jake certainly wouldn't bring his father up for the sake of a punch line.

"He's the one who made the decision," he informed her.

"You're serious." She tried to wrap her mind around it. "He must not have heard about me and Travis yet."

"Oh no," Jake said. "He heard. He still picked you."

That was a different kind of unbelievable. "Where's the loyalty in that? Travis has your dad's back on everything."

"With my dad, business comes first," Jake said plainly. "It always has."

Maya couldn't even imagine her dad doing anything like that. Or what it must've been like for Jake to grow up with that.

She felt bad for Travis, but she also couldn't deny the awe-someness of this opportunity.

"You should be excited," Jake said, reading her mind. Given the permission, Maya smiled huge.

"I could be in a movie," she said. "Oh wow!" She needed to tell people. Immediately. She took Jake by the hand and dragged him inside.

Nicole was in the living room in the middle of downward-facing dog.

"Where's Renee?" Maya asked.

"She's not here," Nicole said. "Why are you frothing at the mouth?"

"I'm on a list to be in a movie," Maya blurted.

"A short list," Jake said.

"A short list!" Maya said. "For the part of a tennis player or something—they're flying me out there to audition."

"Congratulations," Nicole said. "When are you going?"

Maya looked at Jake. "When am I going?"

"I have no idea," Jake said.

"I have no idea!" Maya said to Nicole, as if that in itself was wondrous news.

Suddenly, one person and one person alone popped into Maya's head. Someone she had to tell this amazing news to above all others, and right away.

"I have to go," Maya said, racing for the door. She stopped and turned back to Jake, kissing him full on the lips. "Thank you." Just like that, she was out the door.

Maya ran across campus, through the quad, and around the baseball field, nearly running down two groundskeepers and a kid on a bike along the way. (If the role in the movie involved apologizing to people while running, she would score it for sure.) Finally, she arrived back at her old dorm.

She reached Cleo's door and knocked, hard.

Cleo answered, woken from her slumber. Maya couldn't wait for her to readjust to consciousness—this news was spilling out of her now.

"I'd say 'guess what?' but there is no way you would guess in a million years, so I'm just going to tell you," Maya said. "There's a movie director looking for a tennis player. The Academy picked just a few girls to audition, and one of them is me. Me! I could be in a movie!"

"That's great," Cleo said, yawning. Then she turned and walked back inside.

Clearly, Cleo was still asleep. Maya would have to work a little harder.

"And the director isn't coming here," Maya continued, letting herself in. "They're flying us out. To Hollywood! I don't know who the star is. What if he's there? What if we're auditioning with him? Could you imagine?" Suddenly Maya was imagining, and it was close to triggering a seizure.

Which made Cleo's choosing that very moment to relace her Converse all the more boggling.

"This is kind of exciting, no?" Maya asked, sitting on her old bed. The slight annoyance in her voice would surely bring Cleo back from wherever she was in this moment.

Or not.

"Why are you telling me this?" Cleo asked. She didn't stop lacing her sneakers.

"Because it's good news?" Maya asked.

"Okay." That was all Cleo said.

"I mean, you share good news with friends, don't you?" Maya asked. "I'm sorry, can you please stop lacing your shoes for one second?"

Cleo stopped. She looked Maya dead in the face.

"When was the last time you were here?" Cleo asked.

Maya tensed. "I've been here . . ." She couldn't think of the last time she was in the room. As she looked around for time cues, she noticed the place was a little different. Actually, a lot different. "Right before you got that," she said, pointing at a guitar propped against the wall.

"It's not mine, it's my roommate's," Cleo said.

"You got a new roommate?" Maya asked. "When did this happen?"

"Last week!" Cleo said. "She quote unquote 'plays' that stupid guitar every night like she's Taylor Swift, singing about all the things boys have done to her—which she probably deserved—and I'd freak out on her, but that would just give her something else to sing about!"

"You never told me you had a new roommate . . . ," Maya said in her defense.

"When's the last time we even saw each other?" Cleo asked. Maya was used to playful banter with her, but this felt different. It felt real. "You abandoned me."

Maya caught her breath. "I didn't abandon you."

"And you did the same thing to Renee," Cleo added.

"How can I abandon Renee when we live in the same villa?" Maya asked.

"Where is she now?" Cleo shot back.

"She's not home," Maya said, hoping that was the only answer she needed.

"I didn't ask where she wasn't," Cleo said, "I asked where she was."

"I . . . don't know," Maya finally said.

"No," Cleo said. "You wouldn't. She's at the pool right now. She's been at the pool every morning and every night for a week trying to get her time down for when her parents visit."

Maya was taken aback. "Her parents are coming here? They've never come here. This is a big deal."

"No kidding!" Cleo said. "All Renee wants to do is impress

them, and you were supposed to help her get her time down and you blew her off. Did she or did she not ask you to help her work the stopwatch?"

"She did," Maya said, growing more undone. "And I did! Once. For a few minutes. But there's a clock there, and . . ."

"Of course there's a clock there—it's a pool!" Cleo was going from angry to furious. "She needed you there. You. I needed you, too. I've been freaking out about this whole Svetlana thing, spending time with her, which need I remind you *you* told me to do. And to this day, you haven't spent a single minute with her. You've never exchanged a single word with her."

Maya's face was getting flushed. Her on-court game was defensive by design; she was good at it, but here she had no defense. She didn't know what to do.

"Did you know Svetlana and I started dating?" Cleo asked.

"I didn't . . . ," Maya said.

"No," Cleo said. "Of course you didn't. I haven't seen you here to tell you. I haven't seen you in class. When's the last time you went? Better yet, when's the last time you went to practice?"

Maya was full-on squirming.

Cleo just looked at her. "What happened to you?"

"I'm still me," Maya managed to get out.

"Listen to you," Cleo said. "You don't even believe what's coming out of your mouth. You're so excited people are talking about you. You think you're somebody now. Who are you? What makes you so hot? What, you're on the cover of a welcome packet? You were on some stupid website? The only reason people know you is because of who you hang out with. And that ridiculous makeover. You slather paint on your face with a spatula, wear someone else's clothes, and walk around like you're all that. Nicole is a clown, but at least she's earned what she's got. You came here to be the best, and all you're the best at is partying and sucking face with the entire Reed family."

Maya's eyes teared up. The truth hurt. But she was dumbstruck by how she'd hurt Cleo. That was something she never wanted to do. Or thought she could do.

"I still want to be the best," Maya said. "I still work hard. I ran this morning. . . ."

"Who runs in full makeup?" Cleo snapped. She started to get dressed in a hurry. "You said you weren't one of those girls who was all surface and stupidity. But you are that girl. You're the poster child for that girl. I thought we were real friends. But you're nothing but a fraud."

Cleo grabbed her sneakers and her bag and bolted, leaving Maya behind. Demolished.

Maya sat with Jake on his couch, her eyes red. She was more upset than she could ever remember being. Because this time it was her fault.

"You can't pop a blood vessel over this," he said.

"Why, because Cleo can't stay mad forever?" Maya asked.

"No," Jake said. "Because your LA tryout is in a few weeks and you can't go in there wearing an eye patch."

Jake was obviously new to the whole soothing thing, but he was trying.

"You were right," she said, her eyes fixed on the wall. "The day we met, I was so excited to be here. I said it was a dream come true. You said give it time. The Academy corrupts. It corrupted your family. And now it's corrupted me. Look at me. Look at what I've become. I'm everything I said I wasn't."

"Yeah," Jake said. "But did the Academy do that, or did you?"

She looked at him. "What are you saying?"

"I'm saying, who worked your image?" Jake asked. "Who ditched your friends?"

Maya sat up. "I can't believe this. You're turning on me, too?"

"No," he said. "I'm seeing you for who you really are, just like you saw me for who I really am. You're not this girl. That's not why I'm with you. I couldn't care less about the hair and the makeup and the Christian Louis Vuitton shoes."

"Christian Louboutin," she said in a small voice. The fact that she even knew that only disgusted her more.

"I'm with you because you've got a conscience," he said. "You've just been lousy at listening to it lately."

He was right. He was absolutely right. She couldn't come up with a defense, because there was none.

"This was all me," she said. "All me. I'm not a victim of the Academy, I'm a victim of myself. I was so down on myself when I got here. All I was being told and being shown was that I was a reject. Less than everyone else. And I started to believe it. I . . . I changed to avoid it, instead of changing the way I was thinking."

She caught a look at herself in a nearby mirror. She pulled at her over-styled hair. Suddenly, the realization of just how ridiculous she looked washed over her like a tsunami. "Oh my God, I look like a moron!"

"You don't look like a moron," he said.

"No?" she asked. Then she yanked off one of her fake lashes. "How about now?"

Jake laughed. "Those aren't your real eyelashes?"

"Nope, neither is this," she said, pulling off the other one. The she unhooked a few extensions from her hair. "None of this is mine—the outfit, the earrings. It's all Renee's. I can't afford this. No one can afford this!" She started wiping off her makeup like a madwoman.

"Okay, you're going to hurt yourself," Jake said. Maya was too worked up to be reasoned with.

"I'm dumping it," she said. "I'm dumping it all. All this Glamazon BS, it's done. This is why your dad put me in the villa. Why he picked me to go to LA. Not because of anything I can do on a court."

"He wouldn't have picked you if he didn't think you could pull it off," he said.

"I didn't come to the Academy to pull something off," she huffed. "I came here to compete. I came here to be the best."

"So you're just going to give up on LA?" Jake asked.

She thought about it.

"No," Maya said. "I may not have earned the opportunity, but I'm going to deserve it. I'm going to do what I came here to do, and that's work my butt off. I'm going to hit those practice courts all day and all night and all day again. I am going to sweat. I am going to bleed. I am going to hurt. I'm going to deserve this."

"I don't think I've ever been more turned on in my life," he said. He pulled her back onto the couch. "You know, I can help you out of the rest of these awful clothes right here and now. . . ."

Once again, Maya put on the brakes.

"This starts now," she announced. She got up and headed to the door.

"Wait, you're just going to leave?" Jake asked, smiling. "What am I supposed to do?"

"I'd recommend a cold shower," she said. "A few weeks' worth. 'Cause I'm going to be a little busy."

Jake shook his head, but he also cracked a smile. "Can I get one more kiss before you leave to conquer the world?"

She kissed him. She kissed him again. Then she walked out.

Chapter 18

It had already been a week. A week of Maya waking up before dawn; spending morning, noon, and night at the practice courts; and then crawling home by the light of the moon. She walked off the courts with bags of ice Saran-Wrapped to her body, she woke up sore, and she went right back out and did it all over again. And it felt amazing.

She was herself. She didn't spend any time getting ready, she didn't raid anyone's closet for the most buzzworthy out-fit. She just brushed her teeth, put her hair up in a ponytail, and left. Kids still talked about her, but this time she was the crazy girl who spent every waking second a sweaty, grimy mess. Maya could deal with that.

Throughout it all, Jake was her cheerleader. He'd bring her lunch or dinner. But he wouldn't stay. His fee was a kiss, and then he was off to leave her be. He knew Maya enough to know this was something she needed to do, and he wanted to support that. It made her appreciate him even more.

Even though she lived with Renee, she never saw her. In that rare moment Maya was at the villa, Renee was at the pool. She was on her own mission. An identical mission. But they were going it alone. Maya left messages for her on the villa iPad, she left voice messages and texts on her cell, but Renee never responded to them. Obviously, she was more than just busy; she was hurt, too. She just wasn't confrontational like Cleo was. Maya might have been suffering in the heat on the courts, but she was also in the middle of a deep, deep freeze.

There was one constant in Maya's life, someone she saw around the clock. That person was Nicole. She was prepping for a tournament coming up in Eastern Europe. It was lucky they were both in prep mode, since Nicole was a familiar face and proved to Maya that life was in fact still going on outside the courts. Nicole brought stories, which Maya gobbled up even more hungrily than the burgers Jake brought her.

"How's Renee?" Maya asked when Nicole showed up to the courts one night. She was in the middle of her third straight hour with the ball machine, which she'd become so skilled with she could teach a class.

"She's fine," Nicole said. "She's around less than you are. I could rent out your rooms for extra cash."

"Has she said anything about me?" Maya wondered. "She's still not talking to me. At least Cleo chewed me out. Renee just faded away."

Nicole looked visibly annoyed.

"What?" Maya asked.

"Nothing," Nicole said as she began her stretches.

"Tell me," Maya said. "Is it about Renee? Or Cleo?"

"Maya," Nicole finally said, "that's great that you're worried about them and all, but they need to get over it."

"They need to get over . . . ?" Maya was confused. "What do you mean?"

"What I mean," Nicole said, "is you're living a different life from them. You're dating a Reed, agents and sponsors are starting to care about you, you're going to be on a plane to Hollywood. . . . Your life is bigger than theirs now. Decisions you make are going to have collateral damage. If they don't get it, they don't get it. Focus on your friends who do get it."

Maya furrowed her brow. "Are you . . . jealous?"

"Jealous?" Nicole scoffed. "Jealous of what?"

"Of my friendship with Cleo and Renee," Maya said. "Are you threatened by it, or . . . ?"

Nicole clasped her hands behind her back and bent toward her toes with a flexibility that was insanely impressive. It also actively prevented Maya from seeing Nicole's face.

"I'm just saying, I understand, you know . . . we understand stuff." Nicole was making no sense. And she seemed to know it. She bent back up.

"It's just . . ." Nicole searched for the words. "I'm surrounded by people every day. Tons of people. I have a bigger entourage than Beyoncé and Jay-Z. I've got agents, managers, lawyers, hangers-on. . . . But if I wasn't Nicole King, would they still be around?"

It was a rare moment of openness from Nicole. And Maya wasn't going to wreck it.

"I don't know," Maya responded. "Would they?"

"I don't know," Nicole said. "And how scary is that? I don't know who my friends are, or even if I can have any friends. I've been at this for so long I don't even know if I can trust anyone." She paused, her next words caught in her throat. "I trust you."

Maya was shocked. But then she thought about it. She thought of everyone in Nicole's entourage, everyone she'd seen her with. And the person she hung out with more than anyone . . . was her. Maya Hart from Syracuse, New York, was Nicole King's best friend.

Maya smiled.

"I trust you, too," Maya said. "And if you trust me, trust me when I say this: you may not have experience with friendships, but just because someone is friends with someone else, it doesn't mean they can't be friends with you, too. Or that they like you any less."

Nicole scrunched her face. She clearly didn't like being emotionally exposed.

Just then, Travis walked by. Nicole exhaled. It was Maya's turn to tense.

"Travis," Maya said uncomfortably. "Hi."

Travis looked over, spotting her. He didn't rush over to her, but he didn't run away, either. Maya would take what she could get.

"I'll let you two talk," Nicole said, picking up on the awkwardness. "I need to go get something out of my locker anyway." She started off, but then Maya called after her.

"Nicole," Maya said. When Nicole turned, Maya just smiled. Nicole smiled back, then left her and Travis alone.

Travis spoke first. "Sorry I haven't returned any of your calls."

"It's okay," Maya said. "I've been getting that a lot lately."

"I was embarrassed," he admitted. "I was hurt, and so I acted like a baby. Worse than a baby. I don't even know who that was under that pier."

"I don't blame you at all," she said, and she meant it. "Travis, I hope you know, I didn't mean for anything to happen with Jake." She needed him to believe this. "I never sought him out, and he didn't seek me out, either. It just kind of . . ."

"I know," he said. "I don't blame you, either, and I don't blame him. It happens, right? I mean, it never happens to me, but . . ."

She smiled. He was making an attempt at a joke. That was a good sign.

"Congratulations on the movie," he said. "Or, you know, the tryout."

"Does it bug you that your dad put me up for it?" Maya asked.

"Nah," he said. Maya looked at him. "Okay, a little. But Nails Reed didn't build this Academy by letting emotions get in the way. He's always three plays ahead—that's what makes him great."

"So . . . we're okay?" Maya asked.

"We're okay," Travis said. He pulled Maya in for a hug. And then kissed her on the lips.

She pulled back quickly. Was this some movie moment where they have their tender good-bye? Or was it a friend kiss that rich people did and she was suddenly weirded out for nothing?

"Sorry," he said. "That was . . . I don't know what that was. Won't happen again."

Maya was just relieved to put this whole thing behind them, so she decided not to make a big deal out of it.

"I better get back to practice," Maya said.

"Okay," Travis said. "See you later."

As Travis walked on and Maya went back to her ball machine, she was ultimately pretty pleased. She had a new best friend in Nicole, and she'd smoothed things over with Travis. One broken relationship repaired. Two to go.

While Maya practiced her backhands and forehands, she also practiced stalking. If Cleo was going to ignore each and every call, text, and message in a bottle Maya sent her way, Maya was going to have to find a way to grovel in person. She showed up at her dorm. At the golf course. At the dining hall. But Cleo was crafty. If that's the way she wanted it, Maya thought, she'd just have to trap her where she couldn't hide. Class.

So Maya showed up for class diligently. Cleo, however, did not. After a week of her being AWOL, Maya became concerned. However mad Cleo was at Maya, she wouldn't jeopardize her scholarship by skipping this much school just to avoid her. Something had to be wrong. So when she saw Mr. Manjarrez outside just after history, she leaped on him to find out what was going on.

"Mr. Manjarrez," she said, "is Cleo okay?"

Maya had jumped in so fast she didn't see he was already in the middle of another conversation. With Nails Reed.

"Oh," she said. "Sorry, I didn't . . ." She still felt absolutely ill at ease around him. She knew how he'd treated her when she was a nobody, she knew how he treated his wife, and she knew how he treated his kids. Maybe Travis and Nails's legion of fans could ignore it, but she couldn't.

"It's okay, Maya." Nails smiled. It wasn't a phony smile. He seemed to genuinely like her. Which made the whole thing even more confounding.

"Didn't Cleo tell you?" Mr. Manjarrez asked. "I thought you were thick as thieves."

"Tell me what?" Maya asked.

"She transferred to another class," he informed her. "Suited her practice time better or something."

"Oh," Maya said. "So she's not gone. That's . . . good." She tried not to show how disappointed she was, but it was obvious. Cleo had rearranged her entire schedule to get away from her. This wasn't going to be a couple of weeks of cold shoulder. This was a long-term thing.

The bell rang. "No rest for the wicked," Mr. Manjarrez said, and before Maya knew it, she was alone with Nails.

"You fly to LA on Friday," Nails said, oblivious to any weirdness.

She managed a smile. "Thank you," she said. "You know, for choosing me. And all that."

"Just represent me well," he said. "Travis tells me you've been practicing hard."

Nails mentioning Travis's name stirred something in her. Feelings she was struggling to keep down. But they were coming to the surface here and now, and there was nothing she could do to stop it.

"He loves you, you know," she said, compelled. "Travis."

"I know," he said.

"More than anyone or anything," she continued. "More than Jake. More than football. Travis loves you. So does Jake. Whatever's gone down between you two, whatever problems you have with each other, it's the truth. He'd never tell you that, but . . ."

Nails eyed her. Maya felt the weight of it.

"You have to be real careful with the people who love you," she said.

"Are you giving me some kind of life lesson, Maya?" he asked. Normally she would've been unsettled by a question like that, especially coming from him. *Normally.*

"You're Nails Reed," she said. "What could I have to teach you?" She slung her bag over her shoulder and poised to leave. "I'm just saying. When someone cares about you that much, you have a responsibility to them. To love them, to protect them. To protect their feelings. If you don't, if you're careless, well . . . you could lose them. I learned that the hard way. I just . . . I just wouldn't want anyone else to go through that."

He studied her.

"Well," she said. "Bye." She turned around and walked off. She had no idea if her words landed with him. But she felt better having said them.

·   ·   ·

Since Maya and Nicole were both leaving for trips the next day, they helped each other pack. For Maya, that meant taking things out of Nicole's luggage that she would certainly not need for a tennis tournament in Eastern Europe. For Nicole that meant cramming so much extra junk in Maya's suitcase that the zipper threatened to burst at any moment. Maya was going to Los Angeles, and she needed to look good.

"Take these," Nicole said, tossing a pair of Jimmy Choos in her bag. "I know you're dressing down and all that, but that doesn't mean you can hit the clubs in sneakers."

Maya took the shoes out. "I'm not hitting the clubs. I'm in LA for one night. And I'm going to need that night to rest up for the tryout."

"But you've never been!" Nicole just didn't get it.

"But think of how many times I could return if I scored this part," Maya said.

As Maya went back to her closet, Nicole sneaked the shoes into Maya's carry-on. "What's Jake going to do without you here to brood over?"

"He's coming with me," Maya said.

Nicole sat up. "Jake is flying out to Los Angeles with you?"

"For moral support," Maya said.

"Maya," Nicole said.

Maya looked at her. "What?" Clearly, Nicole had something on her mind.

" 'What'?" Nicole repeated. "You. Jake. Away for the weekend together on a romantic getaway . . ."

"This isn't romantic," Maya said. "This is work."

"Why can't it be both?"

"I mean, it'll be romantic because we're together," Maya said, fumbling. "We're flying there together, too, so . . . there's that. . . ."

"You've come close to sealing the deal a couple times, right?" Nicole asked.

" 'Sealing the deal'?" Maya asked. But they both knew she knew what Nicole meant.

"If you've been waiting for the right opportunity with Jake," Nicole said. "I'm just saying."

Nicole wasn't just saying anything Maya hadn't already been thinking about. Nonstop, in fact. Minus his quick trips to the courts to bring her rations, she'd barely seen Jake over the last few weeks. And that time apart had shown her how much she really cared about him.

"It's just . . . I've never . . . ," she said. "With anyone and . . . it's such a big deal, and I want it to be special and . . ."

Nicole needed to throw her a lifeline. Quick.

"Do you love him?" Nicole asked.

Maya didn't want to just throw out a reply. She wanted to really think about the question. But she already knew the answer.

"Yeah," she said. Then she smiled hearing herself say it. "Yeah, I do."

Nicole smiled, too. "Does he feel the same way about you?"

"I think so," Maya responded. "I think he does."

"So what's stopping you?" Nicole asked.

What is stopping me? Maya thought. Nothing. Nothing at all. She did love him. And he would be good to her. Take care of her. He wasn't the Jake she'd always assumed he was. The Jake who he might have even used to be. He wasn't just with her for sex. He hadn't pressured her this whole time. He waited for her to come to him, to be comfortable.

Maya looked at Nicole. It was a look that said one thing, and it was unmistakable. She was ready. She was ready to go all the way with Jake. The idea didn't freak her out.

This was happening.

Chapter 19

As the plane made its descent into Los Angeles, Maya gazed out of her window in disbelief. How could any city be this big? How could that many swimming pools exist in one place? And how close could you fly to a freeway without actually scraping the roofs off cars?

Maya had her hands full. Or hand. Jake was right by her side, and he was holding on tight. He said it was because he missed her so much, but his sweaty palm betrayed his vicious fear of flying. She loved that he needed her support, and she was more than happy to give it. Because that's all he'd been giving her for weeks. And this weekend she was going to show him how much that meant to her.

Of course, she'd have to tell him first. And she hadn't quite gotten around to that. Having sex for the first time wasn't exactly airport-security conversation, or liftoff conversation, or something to chat up over the safety demonstration. It was also, apparently, not baggage-claim conversation, or waiting-for-the-town-car conversation. But as they drove up La Cienega Boulevard en route to their hotel, time was running out. Maya had to drop Jake off and run a few errands. Tonight was the night, and it was probably something he'd want to be in on.

"You look amazing," Jake said. "I know I said it before, but . . . just look at you." It was true. Maya had ditched the Kabuki makeup and replaced it with a newfound confidence. And she wore it well. She was also in the shape of her life, having been on that practice court 24-7. She was a new girl, again. But this one, she liked.

"You just missed me, that's all," Maya said as she tugged on his T-shirt. It was white with a giant bar code. If he was for sale, she was buying.

"Can't argue with that," he said, pulling her in for a kiss. "But something else is on your mind. It's been on your mind the entire flight out here."

Maya stared at him. She could never get over how in her brain he was. It was sexy and scary at the same time.

"You're still thinking about Cleo and Renee," he said. "They'll come around—I have faith."

Okay, maybe he wasn't 100 percent in her mind.

"No, that's not it," he said, correcting himself. "It's about me." What was he, a witch? "Are you having second thoughts about me? Did you not want me here?" When her face shifted, he started to panic. "That's it, isn't it?"

"No," she said.

"It is, your face totally changed." Now she really had no choice. It was either tell him or watch him completely implode.

"Okay, I'll tell you," she said. "It is about you. And it is about coming to LA. But it's not what you think. Being away from each other, I . . . It made me think about stuff and . . ." All she could do was just say it. "I'm ready."

"Ready for what?" When she didn't answer, he began to clue in. "Ready. Ready? Like . . . *ready* ready?"

"Like tonight ready," she said.

As they pulled up to the hotel, he was speechless. After the driver put the car in park, Jake threw open the car door, hopped out, and reached his hand back to help her out, too.

"Why wait?" he said. And he was dead serious.

"Jake!" Maya laughed, embarrassed. "You know I have errands to run first."

"I'll be quick," he said, smiling. He really was awful.

"I've got to go," she said. "I'll meet you at your room later?"

"Fine," he said, grabbing their bags. "See you tonight."

His words shot up her spine. He closed the door, then banged the roof for the car to drive on.

As she was driven away, she looked back to see him wave. Then he scurried inside. Even though he had all the experience in the world, he might've been just as nervous as she was. And she liked it.

In LA traffic, it took an hour to travel what would have taken twenty minutes anywhere else. Maya didn't mind. It gave her plenty of time to gawk at the sights, and, even more important, the Academy was paying for the ride.

Maya's first stop was the movie director's office. She had

to pick up something called "sides" for her audition tomorrow. She didn't know what the role actually was, but she hoped she got the guy in the end.

Gaining entry to the studio lot where the director's office was located was almost as hard as clearing security at the Academy, but once inside, it was worth every minute. Every minute of the wait, every minute of the plane ride there, and every minute on the practice court the last few weeks on top of that. She'd never seen anything like it.

As she strolled the backlot, she went from being outside the hospital of her favorite medical show (the one where they're saving lives one minute and hooking up in the supply closet the next) to ambling down the faux streets of New York, all in the blink of an eye. She turned a corner and—boom—she was face-to-face with a masked killer who had a machete in one hand and a large coffee in the other.

"Excuse me," the killer said. But instead of a burly guy behind the mask, the killer was an Australian woman. It was official: nothing in Hollywood was as it appeared.

Finally, Maya reached the director's office. She made her way inside, where she found the director's development executive (whatever that was) hard at work in his office. With his hair slicked forward and his hipster bow tie, he couldn't have been much older than she was. He was the entertainment equivalent of Maya—young, gifted, ready to break out.

"Hi, I'm Maya Hart," she said. "I'm supposed to pick up 'sides'?"

"You're a hooker?" the executive asked.

"I'm a . . . what?" Maya was taken aback.

"You're reading for the part of the hooker?" He started thumbing through pages.

"No, I'm reading for the tennis player," she said. "I'm from the Academy?" As he switched piles of papers to look through, she couldn't help but wonder what, exactly, screamed "hooker" about her.

"Here you go," he said, handing her a single sheet of paper.

"What's this?" she asked.

"Your lines," he said.

She looked it over. *Lines* was a technicality. There were three lines, but it was one sentence. How was she supposed to get the guy with one sentence?

"This is all I'm supposed to say?" Maya flipped the paper over in case she missed any more on the back. "How many lines does the hooker have?"

"Eighty," he said. "If we wanted a real actress for the tennis player, we'd have gone through a talent agent."

Well okay, then, she thought. "Hope I can remember these." She smiled, hoping she could wrangle at least a polite grin back. He gave her nothing.

Suddenly, another guy entered the office. He looked at the executive and sneered.

"Jimmy, why are you at my desk?" the guy asked. "And where's my lunch?"

The wunderkind in the bow tie melted into a puddle of subservience. He wasn't an executive after all. He was like Maya, all right, but the Maya she used to be. The wannabe.

"I'll get it right now, sir," the kid said.

Maya showed herself out. Literally nothing was what it seemed here.

As she made her way off the lot, she passed a haunted hotel, two cowboys on their iPhones, and what looked like a middle-aged executive having a breakdown in her car. As surreal as it all was, she still couldn't take her mind off the one thing that was real in the whole city. And that was the guy waiting for her back at the hotel.

Before she could go back, she had one more errand to run. A secret errand she didn't tell Jake about. One that, according to Nicole, would either help set the stage for a night to remember or—if she failed—leave Maya sobbing like that lady in her car.

She needed to hit up a lingerie store.

Maya had told Nicole she was done with the whole dress-up thing, but according to Nicole, lingerie was different. She needed to be sexy for Jake. She needed to be seductive. She needed to not show him her supply of raggedy old bras Nicole was tired of seeing in the laundry.

Maya was pretty sure Jake would be thrilled to see her in anything, but Nicole was insistent. She had a place Maya had to try, a lingerie shop to the stars. They'd hook her up with something amazing. The one catch was that it was on the other side of town.

Maya had the town car take her from Burbank to Malibu. When she arrived, she found a boutique so exclusive there wasn't even a sign. It didn't even look open. But then a woman opened the door.

"You must be Maya," she said in a French accent. "Welcome."

Maya was immediately greeted by more lingerie than she'd ever seen in her life. So many styles, so many colors. She didn't know where to begin.

"What's the occasion?" the woman asked.

What's the occasion? How many different reasons could there be to wear this stuff? Regardless, Maya had no intention of sharing her personal business with a total stranger.

"Just looking," Maya said.

The woman's smile faded. She clearly enjoyed reveling in the juicy details of her customers' lives, and Maya withholding them was nothing short of a personal rejection. "I'll be over there if you need me," she said, retreating to the back.

Maya checked out the merchandise. She wanted something hot. Or, she thought, did she want sophisticated? Or did she want cute? As she walked around the shop, she was hammered by all the options. Was she a stripey girl? Was she lacy? Was she . . . pink? Was that what this color was? And why was it different from this pink, and this pink? One misstep and she'd find herself looking like a hooker after all.

In this moment, Maya wished more than anything that she had Renee and Cleo there to help her. Or save her from herself. She took out her cell to call them, but her battery was dead.

"Looks like someone needs a little help after all. . . ." The woman reappeared, smirking. "Now, why don't you tell me what you have planned. . . ."

She had Maya at her mercy, and they both knew it. Maya

swallowed hard as she prepared to tell this random woman every embarrassing detail of her night ahead. . . .

By the time Maya made it back to the hotel, it was night. She'd wound up choosing a demure cream-colored bra-thing, which she'd changed into at the shop. Even though she was wearing a blouse and a black jacket over it, she was still paranoid people would know she had it on.

Maya checked in and went straight to Jake's room. She'd been gone all afternoon and Jake was waiting. Would he have some little setup going? Dim lights? Room service maybe?

She arrived outside his door and knocked. Suddenly, her heart raced. On the other side of this door, she thought, was literally the other side of her life. After tonight, she would never be the same. Thinking of Jake, she smiled. She was ready. She knocked again.

Finally, the door opened. But it wasn't Jake Maya was facing.

It was Nicole.

Maya smiled, confused. "Nicole, what are you doing here? What happened to your tournament? You were supposed to . . . ?" Nicole was wearing an oversize white T-shirt with a giant bar code on it. Jake's.

Maya looked past Nicole. Jake was in bed behind her, shirtless and wasted. He didn't know Maya was there. He barely knew he was there.

Maya was dumbstruck.

"Tournament?" Nicole asked. "You must've misunderstood. I'm here for the audition."

Maya just stared at her.

"Oh," Nicole said, "I didn't tell you I was on the short list for that part, too? Hm. Must've slipped my mind."

Just then, Jake sat up in bed. "Look who's here," he said, slurring. "It's Maya. Did you have a good day, Maya? I had a good day. I had a friggin' great day." His eyes were unfeeling, but it was from more than just the alcohol.

Nicole smiled. "I hate to be rude, but we're in the middle of something."

With that, Nicole shut the door in Maya's face.

Chapter 20

Underwater. That's where Maya had been, from the minute Nicole opened the door to Jake's room until this minute, when she stepped inside the tennis stadium for her audition. She didn't know how she'd gotten here. She didn't even know how she got back to her room last night. All she could see in her mind was Jake and Nicole. Jake and Nicole. *Jake and Nicole.*

The more Maya tried to make sense of it, the more confusing it got. Every question spawned five more. How could they have done this? To her? And like that? Maya didn't just discover them—he'd known she was coming. And when she got there, no one apologized. They didn't fumble around for their clothes in a panic and promise that it wasn't what it looked like. It was like they wanted her to find them. To suffer.

Everything Maya believed was a lie. Nicole King was her friend. Jake was her boyfriend. They would never hurt her. All of it evaporated. More like blew up in her face. Now all she felt was numb.

The stadium was empty except for the director, his assistants, a camera guy, and the handful of other girls auditioning. There was one familiar face, one that should've blown her away.

Peyton Smith. He was the star in her drive-in movie. She should've been excited. She should've been a lot of things. Instead she was just numb.

"You're late, Maya." It was Bow Tie the intern. He wrangled her down to the court. "You were supposed to be here twenty minutes ago."

"Traffic." It was all Maya could say. This intern who'd played such a starring role in her day yesterday was an extra to her today. She was full-on out of body.

"Nice to meet you, Maya," the director said as she was brought in front of him. "Nails only says great stuff about you." Then he looked her over. "You sure dressed up for us today."

Jake had taken Maya's bags to his room. Since there was no way she was going to go back and get them, she was forced to wear the same outfit she had on yesterday. And that included the lingerie underneath. She didn't even think to change out of it, she was so distraught.

"Thanks for having me," she managed.

"You're going to be reading with Peyton—I'm sure you know him." The director ushered Peyton over.

"How're ya doing," Peyton said. He was one of the hottest young actors on the planet, but to Maya, in this moment, he might as well have been a tree stump with sideburns. She used to swoon over Peyton. She believed he was every romantic character he ever played. Now she wondered what secrets he hid. How many girls he faked into thinking he was theirs and theirs alone.

Before Maya knew it, she was standing on the baseline of the court, racket in hand.

"Peyton will say his line," the director said. "Then you'll say yours, then you'll hand him your racket, and finish it up by helping him swing."

Maya nodded before she could fully process what he was telling her.

"I will never get tennis," Peyton said to her after the director walked away. "It's a ball and a stick. How hard could it be?"

"If anyone can do it," Maya snapped back, "why did you guys fly me all the way to stupid Los Angeles to try out?!"

Peyton looked at her, confused.

"Cut!" the director yelled.

Maya looked up. The director had called "action"—that was the scene he was doing. She was mortified.

"Joke," Maya said, trying to cover up her mistake. "Just cutting the tension."

The only tension was the tension that had been slowly devouring Maya over the last fourteen hours. And it wasn't done with her.

"Going again," the director said, nonplussed. "Action!"

"I will never get tennis," Peyton said again. "It's a ball and a stick. How hard could it be?"

Suddenly, the stadium filled with silence. And more silence.

"Cut!" the director yelled.

"I'm sorry, I'm sorry," she said. "I just . . . I went blank. Sorry, it won't happen again."

But it did happen again. And again. She was so out of sorts that she also forgot to hand over her racket when it was her cue, she looked directly into the camera three times, and she called Peyton by his real name twice. Her only hope of salvaging this trip was nailing the footage of her playing that they were shooting after the scene. But they never even asked Maya to do it. She bombed.

She might as well have walked from Jake's hotel room door to the airport.

As Maya collected her tennis bag, a flurry of people swept in. It was Nicole and her entourage, her agent, Jordan, by her side. Upon seeing her, Maya clenched everything that could be clenched in the human body.

Nicole looked every bit as at ease as Maya was wound up. Nicole was ready to nail this audition. And she was ready to nail it now. Maya wanted to scream. Or run. But she was compelled to hang back and watch.

Nicole didn't need any introduction to Peyton; they knew each other already. The director prepped Nicole in no time, then called "Action!"

"I will never get tennis," Peyton said to Nicole. "It's a ball and a stick. How hard could it be?"

Nicole smiled. "You think you know everything, but you'd be surprised what a girl like me can teach a guy like you." She put the racket in his hands, put her arms around his body, and then swung for him. When they finished their swing, they were turned to where their lips were nearly touching.

"Cut!" the director called out. "Fantastic, Nicole." Maya had to admit it was fantastic. If it was possible, Nicole was almost a better actress than she was a tennis player.

"That whole thing where your faces met up afterward," the director said. "That was some amazing improv."

"I was inspired," Nicole purred, looking at Peyton. She had both men wrapped around her finger.

Anything Nicole had to do after that was a formality. She got the part, and all the other girls knew it. When the director announced Nicole's name, the only one who acted surprised was Nicole herself, and even that was convincing.

As the crowd dispersed and Nicole's entourage conferred with the director, Nicole was left to gather her things. Things that just happened to be at the bench right where Maya had stopped to linger.

"You really shouldn't get down on yourself too hard," Nicole said, packing up her bag. "I've laid out a lot smarter girls than you a lot easier. You at least took a little effort."

Maya just looked at her. What was she talking about?

"From the minute that photographer wanted to take pictures of you after our first hit," Nicole continued, "I knew I had to keep my eye on you. But, you know, there are plenty of cute girls at the Academy. I wasn't concerned. But then you had to go and start dating Travis. By the time Nails moved you into the villa, I had no choice. You were a threat. So I did what I do to anyone who offers me even the slightest hint of competition. I reel them in, learn their weaknesses, and then use those weaknesses to crush them."

"Crush them?" Maya asked, finally able to speak. "We weren't competition. We were friends."

"Were we?" Nicole asked. "Really?"

"Yes, really." Maya wasn't going to let Nicole get away with reimagining their relationship. "We went to parties together, we practiced together. . . ."

"Ever hear the expression 'Keep your friends close but your enemies closer'?" Nicole asked.

"You said you were surrounded by people who wanted things from you, but I was the one you trusted. You told me that!" Maya felt her emotions start to come out.

"That was good, right?" Nicole said. "I almost managed a tear on that one. So close."

Maya couldn't believe what she was hearing.

"You also said I should have sex with Jake," Maya said, her voice small.

"I was right, you should've," Nicole said, zipping her bag and looking at Maya for the first time. "He was fantastic."

Maya was rigid.

"Sorry, Maya," she said. "There can only be one queen bee at the Academy. And it's not you."

With that, Nicole walked off to the open arms of her entourage, who heaped congratulations on her. And after fifteen straight hours of numbness, finally, Maya broke down in tears.

Looking at all the love Nicole was being smothered with, Maya had to get out of there. She couldn't stand all this fakeness. She fled into the stadium in search of something. Something real.

She needed her friends.

Maya pulled out her phone and was reminded again that it was dead. So she made her way to a nearby pay phone and dialed. When Cleo didn't answer, she tried Renee. It just rang and rang. Finally, Renee's voice mail kicked in.

"Guys," Maya said. She could barely spit out words. "I don't blame you for not answering. I don't blame you for ignoring me. I was a jerk. I know I was a jerk. I just wish you two were here, even if it was only to tell me how much of a jerk I really am. . . ."

"You are a jerk," a voice said behind her. Maya turned.

Cleo was standing ten feet away.

And Renee was right next to her.

"What . . . ?" Maya dropped the phone. "What are you doing here?" Maya could see Cleo and Renee, but she couldn't believe they were really here.

"I found out Nicole was auditioning for this thing, too," Renee said. "The fact that she never told either of us, well, I knew something was up."

"We tried to call and warn you," Cleo said.

"My phone's been dead since yesterday morning," Maya said. And then she realized. "You two flew all the way out here . . . for me?" Maya's eyes welled up as she smiled.

"Don't get all stupid," Cleo said. "Renee paid for it, not me."

"We saw the whole thing," Renee said, referring to the audition. "And heard what came after. We were right over there." Renee motioned to seats on the other side of where Maya and Nicole had spoken.

Maya started to cry again.

"I'm so sorry," Maya said again. "I was a beast. Cleo, you were absolutely right. I was not there for either of you at all. I got what I deserved."

"Nobody deserves what Nicole did to you," Renee said. "Did she really hook up with Jake?"

Maya couldn't even say the words.

"Screw 'em," Cleo said forcefully. "Screw 'em both. Who needs them? They weren't your friends. Not your real friends, anyway.

"You look good," Cleo said. It was the first time she'd seen Maya out of the makeover.

Maya smiled. She didn't care if Cleo would freak out. She was going to do what she needed to do. She grabbed Renee and Cleo and hugged them. Hard.

"Oh, come on!" Cleo said, trying to push Maya off.

But Maya just held on tighter.

Back at Renee and Cleo's hotel, Maya watched as the girls packed their suitcases. Renee could've fit a hundred of Cleo's overnight bags into her twelve-piece luggage set—and still had room for Cleo herself.

"Renee, I can't believe I missed your parents coming," Maya said. "I can only imagine what that must've been like."

"Me too," Renee said. "They never came."

"What?" Maya asked.

"My dad had an ambassador emergency," Renee said, zipping her luggage hard.

"What does that even mean?"

"It means they have to come next month instead," Renee said.

Maya and Cleo exchanged glances.

"No matter how hard I try," Renee said, "I'm never going to be good enough for them." It was an awful realization. But it would've been more awful if any of them had tried to deny it.

"Well," Maya said, "maybe you should stop trying?"

Renee took that in. She smiled. "Maybe." But it was easier said than done.

Maya turned her attention to Cleo. "Okay, so. Svetlana? Wedding bells?"

"I broke up with her," Cleo said.

"You . . . ?" Maya just squinted. "Well, that didn't last long."

"It didn't feel right after all," Cleo said.

"So you're not bisexual?" Maya asked.

"No, I'm not," Cleo said. "I'm gay. It was just Svetlana I was torn about. Turns out she was incredibly annoying."

Maya laughed. "That's . . . great? At least now you know?"

"Oh yeah," Cleo said. "Now I know for sure I have something concrete to freak out about."

"Okay," Renee said. "You're a freaked-out lesbian, my parents don't care if I live or die, and Maya's boyfriend cheated on her with one of her best friends. We are in awesome shape."

"So we're a mess," Maya said. "At least we have each other to help figure it out, right?"

Cleo looked at her. "You have to be the corniest person I have ever met."

Maya threw a pillow at her. Then another. And another.

The room phone rang. Renee answered to find their limo to the airport was ready and waiting.

As they grabbed their bags, Renee stopped suddenly. She turned to Maya. "How are you and I going to live under the same roof with Nicole now?"

"Wow, that's amazing," Cleo said in a tone that said she appreciated the entertainment value.

"You're on your own with that one." Maya smiled wistfully.

"Are you moving out?" Renee asked.

"Yes!" Cleo said, thrilled. "Now I can get rid of my roommate. She's one soft push from packing her bags anyway."

Maya didn't laugh. In fact, she was downright maudlin.

"I'm going to help you guys with all your problems, I swear," Maya said. "I'm not going anywhere. Except . . . I am."

Cleo and Renee looked at each other, confused.

"Where are you going?" Renee asked.

It was as hard for Maya to say as it was for them to hear. But she'd made up her mind.

"I'm not cutthroat enough for the Academy," Maya said. "So I'm leaving. For good."

And just like that, their journey together was over.

Chapter 21

As fast as Maya packed to come to the Academy, she packed even faster to leave. She did not want to be at the villa when Nicole got back. Worse, what if Jake was with her? As upset as she was at Nicole, Jake's betrayal hurt her at a level too deep to comprehend. She could at least pretend to understand how Nicole could've gone after her the way she did. But Jake . . . To make someone fall in love with you out of sport, to prey on her heart as part of some game, was inhuman. Nicole might have almost managed a tear that night on the tennis court, but Jake had sobbed in her arms. All to get some play. He was a monster, and the mere possibility that he could walk through that villa door before she could leave made what was left of her heart pound out of her chest.

"It's true, then," he said. Maya turned to see him walk through the door. It was a Reed, but not the one she feared.

Travis. And he didn't look happy seeing her throw clothes in a garbage bag. He didn't look happy at all.

"You can't go," he said. "Not like this."

"Throwing all my crap in a garbage bag isn't the big romantic exit?" Maya asked. "I've had my fill of Hollywood. This is reality, right here. Plastic drawstring and all." She examined a pair of her sneakers, worn down from weeks on the practice court. Instead of packing them, she just chucked them in the trash.

"He really hurt you," Travis said.

"He really hurt me," she answered without hesitation. "You know, the whole time I knew. The whole time I said to myself, this guy is a player. Be careful. Even you warned me, and you're his brother. But I ignored it. I ignored you. I gave him the benefit of the doubt. And now look." She picked up a welcome packet. The packet with the picture of her on the cover. She tossed it in the trash, too. "The joke is on me."

"Maya," Travis said, stopping her from packing if just for a moment. "You're not the first girl who tried to change him. But Jake . . . he'll always be Jake. I'm just . . . I'm so sorry you had to find out this way."

"Yeah, well . . . what can I say," Maya said plainly.

"Say you'll stay," Travis said. "I want you to stay. With me."

She looked at him, surprised. But touched. "Travis . . . why would you even want me to? I chose him over you. I hurt you."

"Maybe I have a psychotic need to clean up after my brother's mistakes," he said. "Maybe I have a compulsive, unhealthy need for you and everyone else in the world to see all Reeds were not created equal. Or maybe . . ." He stepped closer. "Maybe everyone makes mistakes, including you. And I just really, *really* care about you."

Maya didn't know what to say. The day she showed up, she'd been so in awe of this gorgeous creature standing in front of her that she could barely speak. She'd felt unworthy, that he was so far beyond out of her league. And here he was today, pleading for her to stay and be with him.

"I want you to know how much this moment means to me," she said. "How much I appreciate it." But then she pulled the plastic drawstring closed on her makeshift suitcase. "But I . . . I just have to go."

He nodded. "Okay, then, Maya Hart," he said. "Good-bye." He bent in and kissed her. Then he walked out, leaving her alone. It was all so bittersweet.

"Good-bye," she said.

Maya had cleared every last item of hers out of the villa. As much as she needed to leave before Nicole came back, she still hesitated. Because what she had to do next was going to completely, emotionally lay her out. But she'd delayed the inevitable as long as possible. She slung her garbage bag over one shoulder, threw her tennis bag over her other, and trudged to her old dorm to say good-bye to Cleo and Renee.

As Maya walked from the villa to Watson, she remembered back to taking this same route but in the opposite direction. When she'd left the dorm to move to the villa. She'd been so overstimulated, like she'd just pounded a quintuple shot of espresso after eating an entire bag of sugar. At the time it felt like she was living someone else's life. Little did she know, she was.

Maya got to Cleo's. By the faces that greeted her, it might as well have been a funeral.

"Yikes," Maya said. "Am I dying?"

"You're not, but I am." Renee was already tearing up.

"Okay, stop," Maya chided her. "You're acting like we're never going to see each other again. If you act like that, that's what I'm going to think. Do you want me to think that?"

"No," Renee blubbered.

"Do you see what you're leaving me with?" Cleo asked. "She's worse than you are."

Maya smiled.

"Just stay," Renee said. But they'd all tried and failed too many times to change her mind. In the hotel, on the plane. They knew what was done was done.

"Stay strong," Maya said, handing Renee a tissue. "This is no place for the weak."

Maya took a moment to look around at her old room.

"Cleo," Maya said, "your side of the room is the exact same disaster it was the day I got here."

"Remember how scared you were of me?" Cleo remembered back fondly. "That was awesome."

"I still am." Maya smiled. Then she looked out the window. "I remember seeing you for the first time, Renee, right down there. You were walking by. Cleo was talking so much smack about you."

"I was not!" Cleo said.

"No, she wasn't." Maya laughed. "I'm kidding. But I do remember thinking how beautiful you were. And how easy your life must've been . . ."

Renee couldn't help but smile at that one.

"I was weak," Maya said. "The day I got here? Woo." Her eyes went from looking out the window to looking at it. Jake breaking it to get her inside felt like an eternity ago.

"I've grown up so much. I learned who I am, who I want to be . . . and who I don't want to be. That's why I'm leaving. This place can bring out the best in people, but it can also bring out the worst. I don't want to risk my soul by staying. Now that I've found it, I kind of don't want to let it go."

"You still suck," Cleo said.

"Plus I made amazing friends!" Maya said overdramatically. "And there's nothing more valuable than that." She pulled Cleo and Renee in for one more over-the-top hug. But this time, Cleo didn't struggle.

Maya made her way through the quad. All that was left to do was drop off her key card and she was free.

"Maya!" The voice was deep and piercing.

Jake.

She sped up.

"I know you heard me!" Jake said, running after her.

"Leave me alone," Maya barked. She couldn't even say his name she was so angry.

"I want my chain back," he demanded.

"Your chain?!" Maya asked. "That's all you care about? Check the toilet of Delta flight two-two-three. You have my luggage."

"The hotel has your luggage," he shot back. "Get it from them."

He really was a monster. He had the nerve to treat her like this after what he did?

"I trusted you," he said. "I thought you had a soul. But you're like everyone else around here. I can't believe you'd do what you did to me."

"What I did to you?!" Maya said.

"You knew how crappy I felt finishing second to Travis my whole life," Jake said, tearing into her. "You knew and you did it anyway."

"What are you talking about?" Maya was completely confused, and this conversation was already going on way too long.

"You had sex with Travis," he said.

"*What?*" Maya said.

"You didn't think I'd find out?" His rage on the field paled in comparison to his rage right here on the quad. "That's why you didn't want to see me all those weeks you were practicing. You were hooking up with him!"

"No," Maya said. She couldn't process what he was saying as fast as he was saying it. "This is insane. I didn't see anyone when I was practicing!"

"Oh no?" Jake asked. He whipped out his cell phone and showed her a picture.

It was a close-up of Maya and Travis. And they were in a serious lip-lock.

"What?" Maya was blown away. Where did this picture come from?

"Nice dog tag," Jake said pointedly. "I don't remember you having that when you guys were together."

She looked at the picture harder. She recognized the fence behind them. Then she realized when it was taken.

"That was from a week ago on the practice court," Maya said. It was when Travis gave her that totally weird kiss.

"You admit it!" Jake said.

"I'm not admitting anything!" Maya shot back. But then it started to fall into place for her. What was really going on. And it made her sick to her stomach.

"Nicole sent you that," Maya said. She didn't need him to confirm it. "She had to have taken it because she was the only one there. Jake, I didn't kiss him; he kissed me. It was bizarre and I couldn't figure it out, but now it makes sense. It was a setup."

"A setup?" Jake said skeptically.

"She said she was practicing for a tournament," Maya said. "She didn't have a tournament; she had the same audition I did. She wanted to mess me up. . . ."

This was the weakness Nicole had used to crush Maya. This had been her plan all along.

"Oh my God," Maya said. "Nicole was the one who put the idea in my head about going all the way with you in LA. She was the one who made sure I was gone all afternoon with that lingerie hunt. She needed time."

"Time for what?" Jake asked.

"When did she send you that picture?" Maya asked. When

he didn't answer right away, she answered for him. "As soon as I dropped you off at the hotel, right? She magically showed up with the picture and the terrible news, and she was there to lick your wounds. How many bottles of vodka did she have tucked in her coat?"

"None," Jake said. "It was gin."

"Don't you see?" Maya asked. "She wanted me to walk in and catch you! She wanted to rip my heart out, to take away the thing that mattered the most to me. You."

Jake was confused. "If that picture was a setup, then Travis would've had to have been in on it. Why would he help Nicole break us up?"

That was the easiest part of all.

"Because he hates to lose," Maya said. "I could be wrong, though. Too bad I didn't know to ask him when he was at the villa a little while ago begging me to stay here and be with him."

" 'Be with him'?" Jake repeated.

"Think about it, Jake," she said. "Which two people does winning mean the most to at the Academy?"

Suddenly it hit him, all at once. "He's as bad as she is. He's worse than she is. I'm his brother!" He got more and more furious. But then he focused back on Maya. "At least now we know. I know you didn't hook up with him. We know this is all their fault! Maya, we can be together again."

He swept her into his arms. But she went stiff. Cold. When he backed off and looked in her eyes, there were tears.

"I'm sorry," she said. "We can't. I can't."

"What do you mean you . . . ?" Jake searched her eyes.

"The damage is done," she said, trembling. "You had sex with Nicole. And when I look at you . . . that's all I can see."

"No . . . ," he said. "I was drunk. I thought . . . She made me think you . . ." She looked away. "Please don't do this. Don't do this, don't let them win."

"Don't you get it?" Maya said sadly. "They've already won."

Jake shook his head as Maya picked up her bags and walked off.

"Maya!" He started to follow, but she just walked faster. "I'm going to get you back, Maya. I'm going to get you back!"

But she kept going, tears streaming down her face. Until she was gone.

Maya walked swiftly toward the Admissions building. She gripped her villa key card so tightly it left a bright purple impression in her palm. Satisfied she'd left Jake far enough behind, she slowed. He might have been gone, but she could still hear him in her head. Calling after her.

She opened the door to the Admissions building. Up ahead was the office where she'd picked up her key on the very first day. On the wall was a framed poster of Nicole. It was different from the one Maya had stolen for her. This one earned Nicole's seal of approval.

Suddenly, Maya's tears of sadness turned into something else.

Rage.

From the second she stepped off the bus, all she'd wanted to do was run. That's all she'd been doing her entire time here. And she was doing it again. Was she just going to keep running? After everything Nicole did to her, after everything she took from her, Maya was just going to let her chase her away with absolutely no consequence?

As she stood at the door to the main office, with the little window just big enough for her to be able to slide through, one word replaced the echo of Jake's voice. "No." No, she couldn't.

She wouldn't.

Maya wasn't the same meek person she'd been when she arrived here. The same person who felt out of place and over her head. Who was so intimidated by everything and everyone around her. Who was so in awe of Nicole King. This Maya had seen too much. She'd lived too much. She'd learned too much.

The receptionist eyed Maya. "Can I do something for you?"

"No," Maya said, wiping her eyes dry. "No. I'm going to do something for myself."

She turned around and walked out of the building. She made her way back onto the quad, back onto campus.

Nicole wanted to know how tough Maya could be? She was about to find out.

Game on.

The game isn't over yet.

Read on for a sneak peek of the next book in

The Academy
series

Maya carefully stepped out of the Porsche Cayenne Turbo, making sure that her skirt didn't ride up too high as she reached for the curb. The line to get into 360 went all the way down the block and every head turned in Maya's direction to see who was getting out of the luxury SUV. She felt like she was disappointing them by failing to provide a genuine star sighting.

Diego slipped out from the backseat. He let out a long, low whistle when he saw the line. "We are never getting in tonight."

"It's okay," Maya said. "Travis is probably on some list. We'll be fine."

Maya sounded like she knew what she was talking about, but the truth was she'd only been to one other hot spot. This kind of atmosphere was almost as foreign to her as Diego's homeland had been.

They waited on the sidewalk while Travis gave detailed instructions to the valet about the proper way to park the car. He wasn't normally so specific, but it wasn't exactly his car that he was about to hand over to a total stranger.

Travis's Mercedes Roadster was only a two-seater. The three of them quickly realized that they would need an alternative mode of transportation after they slipped out of the formal reception unnoticed. Since Maya was carless and Diego's limo had gone off duty, that only left one of the rides in Nails Reed's small fleet of vehicles. Quietly slipping out of the garage in a car stolen from his dad's collection was Travis's second act of rebellion that night.

When Maya turned her attention back to the club, she was surprised to see the bouncer holding the velvet rope open for her. "Good evening, Ms. Hart. Welcome to 360."

Maya looked down at the rope then up at the bouncer. "Excuse me?"

"Ms. Ledecq is already inside," he said. "She made sure you were on the list."

"Th-thank you." Maya stepped across the invisible line separating her from the riffraff waiting on the sidewalk. It wasn't the first time she had gotten past a velvet rope, but on the previous occasion she'd had Nicole King by her side.

"Impressive, Maya," Diego said as he followed. "You do know how to show off for the new guy."

They waited in the doorway beneath the neon 360 sign for Travis to catch up. "I figured there was a chance Renee put us on the list," Maya said. "But I didn't have to tell him who I was. He *recognized* me."

Diego smiled. "Of course he did, Maya. You're news. I was reading blogs about you all the way in Rio after that tournament."

"But . . . I didn't even win." The fact that Maya had made news wasn't news to her. She'd seen the articles herself. She just didn't think anyone else had seen them.

"Why are you hanging out in the doorway?" Travis asked when he finally caught up to them.

"Maya wanted to make sure you could get in," Diego joked. "Since we're clearly not celebrities like her."

"Speak for yourself." Travis took Maya's arm. "I'm the son of Nails Reed, football hero. That makes me famous by association . . . able to get into clubs across this nation . . . so long as the owners remember my dad."

Maya laughed along with Diego even though she thought she'd heard an unusual touch of bitterness beneath Travis's joke. She expected that type of attitude from a different Reed brother, not Travis. Brushing it aside as a figment of her imagination, Maya walked through the doorway and into an entirely different world.

The club was thumping. Music pounded out of the speakers and lights danced along to the pulsing beat. Bodies filled every inch of the floor. Most were moving to the rhythm, but a few were completely out of step and didn't seem to care at all.

Maya felt like she had *arrived*, entering on the arm of a hot guy. Sure, they were only friends, but the girls shooting her jealous looks as they watched the entrance for potential dates didn't know that.

The good feeling lasted for about half a second—until she saw that other brother heading their way. This city might be a lot bigger than her hometown of Syracuse, but it could just as well be a tiny village for the amount of times she ran into Jake Reed.

"What's the matter?" Travis asked as she pulled away from

him. He held on tighter, unaware that his brother was coming toward them. "It's okay. Friends can hang on to each other's arms. It doesn't mean anything."

"No," Maya said. "It's—"

"I thought you two had some official hosting duties tonight. Did Dad give you a 'get out of fancy reception free' card or something?" Jake may have been speaking to both of them, but his eyes never once looked to Maya. If only the same could be said for other eyes in the club.

The death glares Maya now got from the girls scoping the entrance almost made her laugh out loud. They must have made for an interesting sight. If only those girls knew the truth. Maya was standing with three of the hottest guys in the club, but it was the last place she wanted to be.

Acknowledgments

Tennis has given me an extraordinary window onto the world. I've seen victory and defeat, drama and comedy, both on and off the court. I've traveled the world and learned about its cultures, and I've met the most spectacular variety of people. These are all the elements of good storytelling—and with that I'm embarking on a new career in fiction, with the help of a lot of very talented and special people. Thank you to all of you.

MONICA SELES was

awarded a full scholarship to a sports academy at the age of thirteen and attended a couple of sports academies during her career. She won the French Open at the age of sixteen and went on to become the number-one-ranked woman in tennis, winning a total of nine Grand Slam titles before retiring from the game in 2004. Monica was inducted into the Tennis Hall of Fame in 2009. She is now an ambassador for the Intergovernmental Institution for the use of Micro-algae Spirulina Against Malnutrition (IIMSAM) and a board member of the Laureus Sport for Good Foundation, using the power of sport as a tool for change. Her memoir, *Getting a Grip: On My Mind, My Body, My Self*, was a national bestseller.

JAMES LAROSA loves drama, but he was too much of a

goody-goody growing up to actually cause any. So he became a television writer, concocting scandalous tales for CBS, NBC, ABC Family, and MTV, among others. He also dug up dirt in sports, interviewing top athletes for *USA Today*, *Tennis* magazine, and Tennis Channel.